MICHAEL BOWLER

WEST HOUSE
CARHAM ROAD,
CAHENSIVETEN,
CO. KERRY
V23 Y 5Y8

TEL: 066 948 1602
EMAIL: MIKEBOWLER@HOTMAIL.CO.U

MOBILE

TWO WOMADS

First Published in 2021

Beyond The Vale Publishing

Michael Bowler

TWO WORLDS

IN MEMORIAM

Pauline Bowler

Amor Ipse Notitia Est

DEDICATION

TO MY SPORTING PALS

Patrick O'Shea (Training pal, Ireland)
Graham Payne (Training pal, England)
George Maybury
Michael Ferry
Jim Gaughan
Pat Bonass
Chuck Foote (America)
Jose Luis De Sousa (Brazil)
Christy Riordan
Pat Healy
Mike O'Shea
Christy O'Connell
Con (Conbus) O'Shea
Lorcan Murphy
Ted Foley
Sean Houlihan
Colette O'Sullivan
Claire O'Connor

Brendan Sheehan
Padraig O'Shea
Mick Traynor
Pat Timmons
Michael Fennell
Joanne Cullen
Frank Reilly
Pat Dobbs
John Kissane
Joe Geogh
Cian Murphy
Tim O' Connor
Niamh O' Sullivan
Annette Kealy
Katie Reidy
Stephen Donnelly
Rod Godfrey
Mickey (Scottie) Scott
Mike Whittaker
Angela O'Shea
Jack Griffin,
Dan (Clahane) O'Sullivan,
Sean O'Shea,
Seamus Hoare,
Martin McEvilly,
Ger O'Shea
Dermot O'Sullivan
Owen O'Sullivan
Brendan King

Niall O'Shea
Carl O'Connell (The Harp)
Padraig Garvey
Peter Grogan
Colin Courtney
Niall Fitzgerald (Fitzie)
Paudie Landers
Dr. Billy O'Connell
Dr. Kieran O'Shea (Bawnie)
Cillian O'Donovan
Liam O'Connell

Acknowledgements

The author would like to thank the following in assisting with the writing of this book:

Sean Houlihan.
Alison Dowling
Richard Edwards
Rochelle Kalwe

PROLOGUE

'So long,' she said, had said. Here at St. Luke's Cross where he was standing, a stranger. People walked down Summerhill, towards the Saturday night city. A couple glanced curiously at the long-haired man, taking in his athletic attire. A green tracksuit glinted in the gathering dusk. Silver fair locks curled over the collar. He stood for a long time ignoring the stares. Stood stubbornly in the chill of a late summer's evening.

Two youths lingered to look at him before one of them sang out.

'That's not a bit o' talent boy, he's a nancy.'

The comment did not touch him as it faded in their scuttling steps. He took one last look at the place he used to stay at as a student. Memories. Regrets.

Halfway down the height he heard some music, distant.

'Oh please,' she said, had said.

The music... so long. Years since the Beatles.

'I Wanna Hold Your Hand.'

I want to hold the hand of time.

How innocent those days, how deep with dreams those endless nights. How can a man be nostalgic for the pain and chaos of adolescence? The lonely loveless summer of soccer in the empty evenings. The harbouring of the foetus soul in the awakening womb of life. Thinking. His mind skips over the playground of his life. Skips but never rests to recall the profound echo of concrete and crayon.

He came to her house, unusually with a name rather than a number. There was what looked like a white star on the blue gate. Her long blonde hair that framed her face, found favour in his mind. He stopped and memories of another Saturday night flooded the silent night.

PART ONE - 1966

Redeem the time; redeem the dream,

The token of the word unheard, unspoken,

Till the wind shakes a thousand whispers from

the yew,

And after this our exile.

T S Eliot

He was nineteen. Silently forging his own identity. Finding and losing his soul in a season. Summer saddened with city solitude. Revising for his exams at University College Cork. Staying with a Protestant family in Adelaide Place. Sharing digs with a boy from Dingle and an orphan from Ennis.

Another solitary Saturday. Waking late in the small bedroom he shared. Sean had already gone; he was training in the Tank Field for a football match. The sun filtered the dust above the door. He was muzzy with memories of last night. The music lingering loud in his ears. Cigarette smoke tangled in his hair. Breath exhaling the bitter after taste of beer. The boys had persuaded him to go to a students' dance in the Arcadia.

The top showband in Ireland were playing. 'Let's do the Hucklebuck.' Girls screamed as the large lead singer lumbered on stage. The dance floor flooded with sweating bodies. The smell of perfume as the girls jigged and jived. Beer breathing lads bundled together after the bars had closed. He had two half-pints, forcing the terrible taste down. In the milling crowd he lost sight of the other two. Alone in a world of colour and chaos. When they played 'House of the Rising Sun' he asked a girl with glasses to dance.

'No thanks,' her words pierced his pride. He reddened and felt the sweat trickle down his face. It could have been tears. Time turned past midnight; he wondered should he wait for the others. He saw Sean on the dancefloor, slowly dancing. The girl had the high complexion of the country. The city ones preserved a paleness even though it was stifling.

He edged towards the door and slipped into the night. The warm residue of the day still lingered. In the dark sky a scatter of stars hung. He walked slowly past the railway station. He was reminded of journeys. The words of a song echoed the ache he felt inside.

'And now that I've found you,
I'll be counting on you,
No man is an island,
And I need you, honest I do.'

He blessed himself passing the back of the church and thought of the blonde-haired girl in Summerhill. He often saw her on Sundays, walking against him as he returned from the church. He wondered did she go to early Mass. He would see her opening and shutting a blue gate with a star in the centre. 'Mizpah' the name above the door of the house. He didn't know what language to attribute the unusual word to.

The landlady had left the light on in the hall and he allowed it for the lads. He lay in bed and the song 'I Need You' and the image of the island was finally submerged in sleep. After a breakfast of toasted Mother's Pride and tea he walked down to the city. A smell of sludge lifted from the Lee as he crossed Patrick's bridge. He stopped at Eason's to buy a history book. Partition. The banjo man was playing outside Roches Stores. A dirty hat sprinkled with silver at his feet. His mangy mongrel sniffing for food on the footpath. He was playing 'The Banks Of My Own Lovely Lee' again. It was nearly lunchtime when he stopped browsing and returned to the digs. There was only Aiden in the dining room, revising over a cup of coffee. He was studying for a B.Sc.; ideas did not enter his head if they didn't have a scientific basis.

The house was silent. A church bell rang out, Liam felt restless. He could not concentrate, wanted to articulate his emotions. Words and music, feeling humiliation. Last night forcing himself to find someone. An island in the dawn. He foraged in the communal wardrobe for a book. He was always swopping with Sean who was reading literature at UCC. The Outsider. He empathised with the title and took a slim volume of poems by Hesse as well.

Out in the dazzling day he turned up towards Mayfield, making for the Glen where he would find some shade. A shallow brook bisected the burnished grass. He sat in the emptiness near the water. He imagined Algeria; became Camus. Turning an indifferent page, he didn't notice the girl. Quietly she walked along the tree strung path by the brook. They were both startled out of their thoughts.

14

'Oh, sorry, I never expected another here.' she half stopped.

He recovered his calm and answered. 'That's alright, neither did I.'

She gave a shy smile and a little laugh. There was a kindling of kindness in her eyes. He encountered uncertainty for a moment. 'There's enough space in the field for two,' he heard himself say.

She hunkered down and place a book between them. 'Isn't it roasting,' she pushed a blonde fringe back from her forehead.

'Dead heat,' he agreed.

An active silence ensued before he spoke again. 'Haven't I seen you before in Summerhill?'

'Probably, I live halfway down there.'

'I'm Sarah,' she said.

'Liam.' They were silent for a moment.

'Still at school?' he asked awkwardly.

She nodded, 'I've just done my Leaving. Honours,' she added.

'What about yourself?'

'Me, I'm at UCC, History,' he also added. They laughed at their emphasis.

'Was it Henry Ford said history was bunk?' she asked.

'More modern mythology,' he dismissed his subject.

'I can learn as much about colonialism from Camus,' he flourished the Outsider.

'Ah, L Étranger,' she cultivated a French accent.

'Isn't that about the absurdity of life and the main characters indifference to death?' she adopted a serious face.

'Or vice versa,' he answered.

15

'Have you lost faith in eternity so?' she said suddenly.

He looked towards the brook. Out of its reflection a stark tremulous tree grew. An oak he'd seen so many times before but never its rootless image of age.

'I can't believe God ever touched the life we know and doubt. He can only look down on our darkness.'

'That's very strange talk,' she replied in a hurt voice.

'Strange?'

'Look at Vietnam; the rituals of revenge in the North,' he got up abruptly.

'Let's walk a while,' he looked down at her.

Green eyes with flecks of gold held his gaze.

She held her hesitancy like a shield before him.

'Yes, alright,' she relented.

She wore an orange tee shirt tucked inside blue jeans. An image of sunsets, homeward hills, Hollywood, parting on a shore pained his eyes. She walked ahead of him, along a narrow trail. The sway of her blue jeans tantalised his sun-warmed senses. The cool shadow of a tree covered her body. She turned; the profile of her tee shirt trembled. A half-smile opened her lips as she leaned a hand against the bare bark. A myriad of emotions clashed in his mind. He wanted to touch her against the tree; he wanted to take her to the stars. Her lips softened for a second as he found himself trying to kiss her. They broke apart abruptly; a silence settled over the Glen.

They walked on past the high bleached grass that bordered the stream. The flat top of the Country Club a white haze above the surrounding green. The day moved on to prepare for Saturday night. Students pooling their pocket money to buy beer before the dance at the Arcadia. Painted factory girls waiting to hurry down from Sundays Well to mingle with the country intellectuals. To mingle but never cross the class barrier. Silence. He wondered if he might see her again. Talk to her.

'The Beatles are on at the Lee,' he ventured.

'I know, I saw the queue for a Hard Day's Night,' she was non-committal.

'What are you going to do for the holidays?' he tried.

'I'm hoping to work with preschool children, teaching,' she replied, 'And what about you?' she asked.

'I'm going home to wait for the results.' Strand during the day, soccer in the evening.

'Passing time mainly but saving hay and bringing home the turf too,' a hint of regret in his voice.

'Where is home?' she digressed?

'Kerry,' he simply said.

'Ah, the Kingdom,' she smiled at the image.

'Anyway, it must be lovely to get away from the city for the summer.'

And they continued to ask questions in turn as they reached the main roads. Fragments he held onto, keeping Saturday night at bay. Without decision they walked towards Saint Luke's cross and goodbye. A number 8 bus laboured past, laden with returning shoppers. The artificial gust in its wake parted her fringe briefly before subsiding. Their shoulders touched. He glanced at her face, but her eyes were silent.

'I live in digs,' he pointed to a tree-lined gateway.

'Don't you get lonely in digs?' she said softly.

17

'Sometimes,' he released one word. 'Why, don't you know the feeling?' he said.

'Living at home?' she mused. 'Not really. Maybe existentially,' she pronounced precisely.

'I expect you'd want to experience the word to know its meaning,' she finished quietly.

He never forgot that phrase. Never.

They stopped indecisively outside the silver railings of Saint Luke's. His landlady went to the Sunday services there. The evening sun deflected gold strands from her hair. The diamond of the day declined in her eyes. Gold, silver and silence.

He held hope for a moment in his hands. The inexorable night calling across the city skyline. Sounds carrying on the faint stirring of a breeze.

'Listen, I must go home now,' she raised her book in salute.

'What's that book,' he played for time.

'Oh, it's called Children of the Dream,' she studied the cover. 'It's about native-born Israeli children, called Sabras,' she added a new word. 'I'll be off to teach on a kibbutz shortly, and hopefully improve my Hebrew,' she added.

Disbelief drained the life from his face. He looked into the green gaze of her eyes in silence, Saturday night opening out in front of him empty.

'When?' He uttered the word like a loss.

'September,' she answered softly.

'I only wanted to see the Beatles with you tonight,' he felt his cheeks flush.

'Oh please,' she implored.

'I couldn't anyway. I am helping some children prepare for Hanukkah; that's our festival of lights,' she explained.

'I didn't realize, I'm sorry... but you don't look ...you know,' he said confused.

'It's alright, this is where colour subverts the stereotype,' she fingered her hair.

'Are you emigrating forever,' he asked calmly now.

'I'm going home,' she said simply. 'Diaspora is a form of disgrace to us.'

'Dangerous too,' she added.

'I understand that I expect exile is agony anywhere,' he agreed. 'But won't you miss Ireland,' he continued.

'Of course, my heart and soul will be in two different countries.' She looked lost for a moment.

'Well, it'll be much warmer in Israel than kibbutz Kerry in September,' he smiled wanly.

'Well, so long now,' she half turned away. 'And God bless, Liam.'

'Goodbye Sarah,' he turned to go. Meaning to bless her but could not bring himself to say 'God'.

She walked slowly into the deepening night and left him gazing into an orange back. Of sunsets and loneliness. Camus and Hesse. He watched her disappear down Summerhill. Standing still for several moments, he felt the night fall fully. He opened the gate and walked up the gravel path. He went to his room without having his supper, gazed out the window and looked down on the neon night. He could see the distant cathedral carving a dark profile in the prison sky. A strange feeling of infinite loneliness surfaced in the evening silence.

Existential? He turned and drew the curtains. The sun declined, the light of day diffused, and he harboured in the darkness.

The boys were going to a students' dance in the Arcadia later. Aiden addled him with enthusiasm, and he consented to go for a drink beforehand. The Shambles was full of students tanking up for the evening. Liam had a pint of Harp halfway to his lips when he saw Sarah in an alcove. Protecting their pints, they edged over. Sarah was in company with a couple of girls.

Sean led the way looking for vacant seats; when a couple drained their dregs, he plonked his glass down. As Sarah looked up Liam lifted his glass, silently saluting her above the din. A momentary embarrassment overcame them before Liam spoke.

'Hello again.'

'Hi,' she smiled shyly.

The lads looked at Liam whilst the girls giggled at Sarah. Liam couldn't remember the names or the nature of the conversation as the evening intensified. Aiden bought a round and Sean helped him at the bar. Sarah's friends sought out the ladies and they were alone.

How did Han...the festival of lights go,' he moved closer.

'Hanukkah? Fairly well, as the kids had eight candles to light.'

'Did you get to the cinema to see the Beatles,' she asked.

'No, not without you,' he blushed.

They were interrupted by Aiden; she was drinking white wine. It must have been getting on for midnight when the girls got up to go. Sarah's friends were also intent on the Arc. They walked out together, back over Patrick's bridge. Sarah left them

20

at the Coliseum to ascend Summerhill. She was slowly walking close to him; there was a faint smell of perfume in the air. The heat of the day still clung to the river breeze. At her house she stopped for another goodbye. When he asked, she told him that 'Mizpah' was a Watchtower in Hebrew. She told him there was a biblical dimension to the name with a quotation.

'May the Lord watch between me and thee when apart from one another.'

'Very apt, like us meeting and parting in a single day,' there was a query in his voice.

'Well, shall we say shalom this time,' her lips curved like a kiss.

'May as well, you've given me a few new words already,' he smiled.

He felt his stomach churn, his mouth drained dry. 'Can we postpone goodbye for a while...talk,' he asked.

'Fine, it's a lovely night for a stroll,' she turned away from the blue gate.

His shoulder brushed against her, but she didn't move away. She smiled 'sorry' and pushed him playfully back. They were building bridges in the dark. Acting with their bodies the young needs of the night. Under a canopy of trees, the silent silhouette of her face turned to him. His hands reached out, called by the expectant part of her lips. Moulding shadow to shadow, the night and their bodies one. Her thin blouse retained the warmth of the day. Restraining the softness of her breasts as they spilled into his hands. Coming apart abruptly at the sound of footsteps. His mouth still full of the feel of her lips.

They talked of Ireland, of Israel. Exile. Loneliness led them past Saint Luke's to their meeting place in Mayfield. He remembered the softness of her voice in the gloom of the Glen. The smell of burnt brown grass. The vapid waves of water. The stillness of the stars above the city. The turning and twinning of two worlds. Liquid light fingering the earth, covering their breathless bodies. An overwhelming tenderness troubled his eyes. Clinging like children in the dark they arose as one. The field fell under a dark cloud as they walked away.

There was no Mass next morning as Liam mulled over another cup of coffee. The din of the dance was echoing in Sean's ears. Aiden was drinking copious cups to remove the bitter aftertaste of beer. Sean told them he had ended up in Bishopstown doing the 'Fucklebuck' with a girl he shifted. Aiden told him he better go down to the church for the last blessing in that case. Liam was silent about Sarah when they enquired, a blush his only reply. They were too late for any blessing and Liam continued down to the city.

The sky was billowing blue. A breeze brushed the sleep from his muzzy head. A Sunday lassitude hung over Patrick's Street. Only the Grand Parade showed signs of life in the congregation of children. He walked around to the South Mall; he thought there might be a synagogue amongst the business buildings. Or was it in South Terrace? No sign of a synagogue or Sarah.

Turning back, he strolled aimlessly down the Mardyke. Her face framed in gold before him. Infatuated with feelings, he found solace in the silence. Meandering for miles he let Sunday slip away. Clouds climbed over City Hall as he walked back.

He exchanged the events of the weekend with the landlady over supper. She told him that Hibs had beaten Celtic in the local derby at Flower Lodge. He had played there with UCC against Glasheen once, revelling in the width of the wings. The cropped grass mimicking a carpet; the ball true on every pass. In his room he looked out the window to where they said goodbye. He felt he had lost her, like reaching out in a dream to encounter a shadow. The thief of time had taken her away. A seed of sorrow took root in the darkness. He mourned her memory like a death. Soon he would depart the city for good. He sat his finals on a blazing blue day. The summer stretched stricken before him.

Out the Western Road he thumbed home; he would come back for his books and clothes later. In every lift that stopped the Beatles blared from car radios.

'Can't Buy Me Love' in Killarney. American tourists thronged the streets. Their loud clothes lighting up the shops. Buying a bygone memory, a personal stereotype.

The comfort of Kerry enclosed him in the hills. Shadows reaching out like fingers of friendship. The cross on the highest peak, a silent sentry against the sky. Evening ebb on the river running by the town. Home. His mother putting on the turf in the Stanley range, even in summer. Tucking into a meal of rashers and sausages and tons of tea.

Afterwards he headed for the bridge where he used to fish as a boy. The stark silhouette of the castle edging the river. The embers of the evening sun scattered along the horizon. Finally settling between the twin peaks above Whitestrand. Old men were hauling pollock in over the bridge. A few farmers finding their way home. Darkness descending, carrying sounds across the water. A voice said 'goodnight.' His room was ready when he returned to the farm. School and university behind him; a future determined by dreams.

The farm looked small and empty after Cork. He had to adjust his attitude. There was hay to save; stooks of barley to bind. The turf had to be footed and reeks built on the side of the dirt road. And in between, Whitestrand sucked at his soul. Some mornings he would cycle to Whitestrand on his father's old Raleigh. The dew would still be dancing in the fields. Sometimes only the Canon, reading his breviary was pacing by the foam. Sounds of summer. Waves washing up on the sand dunes. Children's voices carrying on the breeze. In a distant meadow the reaper and binder could be heard. Outboard engines whirring on the river. Solitary summer.

He burned rubber on the Raleigh. Walked the wilderness of the wood. Climbed the hill above Whitestrand. Only sheep and silence clung to the furze coated summit. He was preparing for exile. Alone.

Instead of going to Mass he loitered on the bridge. The Sunday calm broken by the Angelus bell. Called to prayer he cultivated indifference. A well of words overflowing in his mind. A lyric of loneliness reflected from the sun shadowed water. The licks of light catching the colours as they changed from blue to purple on the hills.

Dylan's song 'The Times They Are A' Changing' tripped through his mind. The music was expressing a universal image. The 'winds of change' were blowing over the land. The turf was now cut by machine. The slean and pike were rusting in redundancy. Tractors were drawing the turf home. The horse was unharnessed and turned loose to idle in fields. Young men grew their hair long and young girls were giddy in miniskirts.

Evenings after harvest; going to the Field for a soccer match. Floating over the clumpy grass. Sweat swimming in the eyes. All Summer, nights when the games were over. Cooling down in the ice-cream parlour. The jukebox like an icon in the corner, surrounded by worshippers. The girls in their summer frocks sitting close together. The boys standing in a huddle pretending to be cool. Emotional alienation. Until the new banker's daughter came to town. Touching her with their eyes when her bare brown thighs showed. The rigid rise of her breasts as she got up to buy a 99. Only raising her eyes to glance Liam's way when he left for the farm. At home and homesick.

Before the next match in the field, he found out that her name was Jackie named after President Kennedy's wife. All the boys took it turn to try and shift her to no avail. He exchanged smiles with her the next time they stood side by side at the milk bar.

The tide was washing over Whitestrand when he made his last trip of the Summer. The wide waves were creeping and crashing to the shore. A solitary car was parked on the slipway; two bikes rested in the shade. One child played on the soft warm sand, alone in a castle without care. A man and a woman sitting on a blanket by the sand dunes. Cattle in a cluster cooling down in a pool. He walked over by the rocks; the baleful eyes of the animals watchful as he climbed up. In his view above the bay, he saw the twin hills rising yellow into the blue. Tracing the rim of the sky with a coarse finger of furze.

The sea shaped the land in a wide curve around the bay. He saw a fair figure coming into his view in the distance. Body balancing on a mossy stone, her tight breasts pointing in profile. Her face thrown back to catch the sun skimming off the water. She was dressed all in blue, like part of the sea and sky. He watched her skip from rock to rock, her hair flung across her face. Frightened to face the cattle she veered up to the patch of grass he was sitting on. Her head rising from the rocks, shining with gold strands. He was swimming in the startled depths of Jackie's blue eyes.

'Hello,' she said quietly, without smiling. 'You gave me a start,' she gave a little laugh.

The lashes fell down over her eyes like a cloud across the sun.

'Sorry, I didn't mean to,' he lifted her eyes with his voice.

She looked down at him, her lips curved over her teeth in a pout.

'May I? I'm puffed out.'

'Of course,' he made room on the green sop.

She sank to her knees in a slow feline fall.

'It's no day for endeavour,' he regretted saying. 'Jackie, isn't it?' he asked.

'Yes, how do you know?'

'Someone in the milk bar, I think. Anyway, I'm Liam. So how do you do,' he smiled.

'Finely out,' she grinned in return.

He laid back and she looked down, her hair framing her face. A bead of sweat crossed her forehead and trickled down her face. He reached up and brushed the drop from her cheek.

Her face was warm and warmer where he touched. Her eyes seemed to widen, and her cheek pressed against her hand. He wanted to be gentle, to pretend it was Sarah. He cupped her other cheek with his free hand and drew her face down. The shadow of her hair fell across his eyes. He could feel the soft perfumed waves against his cheeks. Her lips were open and moist as they descended to his mouth.

His hands left her face and pulled her shoulders against his chest. The length of her firm soft body lay on top of him. Her pointed breasts flattening on his chest, her thighs between his open legs. His hands played up and down her back as they kissed. He opened her teeth with his tongue, deeper and deeper exploring her moist mouth. Without taking his mouth away he turned her on her back. He could feel the hardening of her breasts through the blue top. His hand found a nipple through the top. She gave a little moan. His hand slipped under the end of her tee shirt. Her bare skin was warm, and his hand burned at the touch of her breast. His body was blazing with her feel when she reached down and stopped his hand.

'No, please don't,' she was near to tears.

He pulled his hidden hand down over her flat stomach and out into the sun. Shame reddened his cheeks as he fell off her, breathing audibly. He couldn't look at her face. No word had been spoken. A bead of sweat on her cheek and his innocent hand reaching out. He wanted to be gentle.

'I'm sorry,' he looked quickly at her.

She was adjusting her t shirt over the top of her jeans. Her breasts eagerly pushing against her blue top. His look lingered until she caught his eye and answered.

'It's not all your fault,' her voice sounded small.

The day had brought changes. He had played with innocence and lost.

Not for the first time, he thought. Like Sarah all over again. The summer of soccer ended, the milk bar emptied, and he never saw Jackie again.

At the end of September, he went back to UCC to avail of career guidance. Teaching and the Civil Service were the main options. He didn't like the idea of any more study at teacher training college. They agreed that the Civil Service was the best idea in the end. He filled out an application form there and then.

He had booked in to Ardagh House B&B in Wellington Road before walking to his old digs. There was a new influx of students in the dining room. Over a cup of coffee and Mikado biscuits they questioned him about university life.

They looked so eager and innocently young. Their shining faces the mirror of a new Ireland. The incestuous society opening out to adore a new deity. The image of modernity moved over the land. Education was the answer to emigration. They wanted to be the teachers, engineers, the physicists of the future. He left them to their dreams after saying goodbye to the landlady.

He thought he saw her on the number 8 bus as he walked down Summerhill. Saw a flash of fair hair fall across her face. He felt an aching emptiness as he passed her house. He conjured her face for company. Young couples were queuing at the Savoy. Students identified by college scarfs promenading in the Grand Parade. Melodeon music squeezed into the air as pub doors opened. He wondered did she still go to the Shambles?

The edge of autumn cut across the Lee. Back up Summerhill he couldn't define the feeling she had created, love and loneliness. He was overwhelmed that their journeys would never converge. They would wander through separate lives; make new friends, marry strangers. The memory of their meeting fading like a film.

When the bus dropped him off at Caragh Bridge the sun was playing on the water. A burnished brown current flowed over the rocks. After the glass and concrete of Cork the hills reflected soft silhouettes on the river. The smell of wild woodbine wafted from Caragh Wood. Bluebells grew damp in the shadow of ditches. Fairy fingers flourished in the coarse grass. Blackberries bulged in the briars.

As he approached the farm the smell of turf ascended into the warm air. The chestnut tree inside the entrance looked bare and barren. Palm trees parade up the lane to the door. He could see his father in the Upper Meadow bent over the thistles. Sunlight glinted on the scythe as he arced it in the air.

The hay was saved in the haggard. The turf was home for the winter. The cows were turned into the Lower Meadow to crop the aftergrass. Only the bullocks roamed over the slough seeking the rough grass. He could see the colours change as the sun swept a cloud from the sky. All the way down to the river the light lingered, then leaped over the land.

He had to travel to Dublin for the Civil Service interview. Near the end the woman on the panel asked him the name for a cow in Irish. Without thinking he answered 'Daisy,' the best milker at home.

'It's bo,' she said primly, fingering her fáinne. He knew he had failed due to his aversion to Irish. When he got home, he told his parents of the outcome.

'Bo me bollix,' his father profaned.

His mother used the Irish word for rubbish.

'You'd have passed with that,' they had to laugh at the absurdity.

He tried the British equivalent and was called for an interview in Belfast. On the train from Dublin, he could not discern the border. On the way into the city the streets were inundated with Union Jacks. There was a queue at the reception of the Europa hotel. It was later to become the most bombed building during the resurgent troubles.

There were two other candidates, a red-faced girl and an auburn-haired boy. He saw their colouring as a danger sign. Rivals. They were both smartly dressed, and he felt drab in his blazer and slacks. Three men in identical suits conducted the interview. One had a Scottish accent which was hard to decipher.

His moment of concern came when the man in the middle referred to his degree. He was overqualified for the clerical post he applied for. In the end they agreed it wouldn't be an impediment. He could be fast tracked to a higher grade. When it came to hobbies, he gave reading and running instead of soccer. After a quip about the two R's and a joke about being good on a fast track it was over.

At the end he was asked if he would be prepared to take up a post in their HQ in Essex. Letters would be sent out to the successful candidate.

The red-faced girl smiled as he crossed the lobby to hail a taxi. He was relieved to leave Belfast behind.

In two weeks, a large brown envelope arrived emblazoned with 'On Her Majesty's Service'. With mounting trepidation, he tore open the envelope. He had an offer of an upgraded post in their HQ, in Essex.

That night after supper he told his parents he would be off to England by the end of the month. His father half joked 'the old Irish will come in handy when you meet John Bull.' His mother went into town next day to buy him new clothes. On the morning he left his father slipped him a wad of notes as they shook hands. Rivets of rain hammered into his face as he waited for the bus.

A grey head looked out the window towards the hills. The shadow of a boy reflected in her empty eyes. The Upper Meadow misted with her memory. A blonde head leaned out of a balcony on a kibbutz. A cold crowd of strangers streamed up from the orange groves. International volunteers.

Waiting. The hand of time reaching out. From a meadow, on a balcony. Lives linked by dancing nights in Ireland. The image of exile overflowing from a baby's eyes.

The bus was stopping and starting along the water swept road. Schoolchildren livened up the morning, chattering and chittering like late swallows. The slow deliberation of farmers' wives delayed the day.

There was a half hour wait in Killarney before the Dublin train shunted into view. They had to change at Mallow where Liam bought a cup of tea and a ham sandwich. The girl serving called him 'sir'.

Settled on the Cork train his mind skipped over the last summer. There was no pattern that he could cut from his life that led to this journey. Faces found and fled his memory as he tried to focus on his future. The famished face of his mother, the still figure of his father in a hayfield. Football friends flying over sunburned grass. Jackie, his substitute for Sarah? The secret smile of his sister, Aine, after a dance.

Cork always made him feel restless with memories. It was here that he first saw Sarah, his heart turning over. Where he first fondled a girl. The limpid look in her eyes as he knelt before her breasts. The warm tenderness of her thighs. He felt he had found his future.

As he had hours to spare before the boat, he put his case in the station locker. For some reason he was compelled to cross the road to Saint Patrick's, his church. He simply sat in the silence. Candlelight licked the faces of statues. The smell of incense saddened him with the image of the altar boy he had been. He tried to pray but the familiar words wouldn't come.

The night had filled in around the city. The streetlights caught the rain when he looked up. The Echo boys were dashing between cars, selling the evening paper. He looked for a cafe to shelter from the rain. A wintery wind cut across his anorak on Patrick's Bridge. He sought shelter in O'Brien's tearoom. He stirred his pot and watched the homeward city empty. He dwelt in the dimness of the cafe as a shower of hailstones riddled the road. He shivered in the warmth, feeling a premonition of pain outside.

He walked slowly back to the station, killing time. The early evening energy had dissipated in the city. Recovering his case, he headed back to the bus station. The case weighed in the wind as he changed hands. The dock was deserted when he arrived. The Innisfallen listed on the disturbed water as he battled up the gangway. A smell of drink and diesel met him as he boarded. He hadn't booked a berth, so he settled on a seat in the saloon. Tucking his case under the seat he looked for the jacks.

The ship started to fill up as it got on for sailing time. The bar opened and he bought a glass of stout. He walked up on deck as the siren sounded for sailing. A cold black sky hid the stars. The water was swept into dark waves as the ship lifted anchor. The wind whipped the hood of his anorak across his face. People came on deck to watch the lights of the city fade. Eyes were softened as the Innisfallen swallowed its exiles.

Sleep came fitfully as restless children hunted up and down the saloon. Time drifted and dragged as the ship ploughed the black sea. Dawn defined the horizon as the coast of Wales awoke. There was a mad dash for the gangway as the ship docked. Liam lugged his case down the stairway to the exit. His eyes ached with cigarette smoke and sleeplessness. People had drawn into themselves by the time they cleared Customs. The train was late arriving, and the station was overflowing. He eventually got a foothold on the step and found a seat by the window.

The train trundled slowly through the dawn dark countryside. Fields flitted past; the white coats of sheep covering the green. The sun was shadowed by the following clouds. The buffet bar opened, and he lurched along the corridor for a coffee and a cheese roll. He felt better after eating and settled back in his seat to survive the long haul to Euston.

He was awakened by the movement of people hauling their cases to the door. A sad black man took his ticket as he swept to the platform. The size of the station overwhelmed him; arrows and exits in all directions. A momentary panic seized him before he saw the sign for the Underground. Hard-lit faces swept past him, fighting for the train doors. People hid behind papers; pages held high like shields.

At Fenchurch Street he bought a terrible cup of tea like 'tay' in the bog. Sullen, silent faces entered the train for Essex like timid shadows.

The grey, grimy flats faded into a leaden sky as he looked out. The flatness of the fields, empty of animals amazed him. Daylight lingered weakly as the sea suddenly appeared. The ebbed tide revealed a swamp of black mud. There was a sudden pain in the pit of his stomach as he absorbed the alien landscape.

The streetlights hurt his eyes as he left the station. He felt the November night like a cold shadow fall in around him. He didn't know which way to turn to find digs. Spots of rain fell on his face as he turned into the High Street.

A cold wind gusted from the estuary, piercing his face. He walked all the way down the High Street searching for signs of B&Bs. He came to a neon lit building; a hotel or ... The Ritz, a cinema isolated at the end of the street. Grove Road. Tired and laden with his case he stopped at the first guesthouse; number 14.

An old leather-bound face opened the door a smidgen. She led him slowly up the stairs to a small room with a sink in the corner. He had to pay a week in advance before she shuffled out of the room. He looked around and shivered in the cold silence. Going to the sink his pinched face paled in the dim lit mirror. He ran the hot water tap; it was edged with cold.

The room closed in around him, imprisoning the image of exile. The cold politeness of the landlady depressed him. She didn't even offer him a cup of tea after his journey. Only the limp leathered hand, held out for the rent. After unpacking he lay on the bed and closed his smoke smelled eyes. Hunger harried his stomach and he ventured downstairs.

He eventually found a cafe on a corner. The Lido; filled with shabby old men sunk over teacups. Solitary. 'The Streets of London'? Couples straining over a word to bridge their aged silence. He sat on a plastic chair; the cold marble of the table touched his hand. The waitress placed the menu on the table. He glanced up to thank her, but her eyes were elsewhere.

He ate his roast chicken and chips, watching huddled shadows hurry past the window. The cold wind swept the rain through the door as people entered. He was finishing his desert, apple pie and cream, when a figure cautiously entered. He was conscious of a change; eyes left the hardness of plates. Liam nodded as the man indicated the chair opposite.

'Hello, is it alright to sit here?'

'No problem, it's all yours,' Liam indicate with his spoon.

'I'm sorry, the problem?' the man stood still.

'None, I mean the chair.'

The man smiled and sat down shyly.

'Sometimes seats are hard to find.'

'I know, and service,' Liam raised his brows as the waitress flounced by.

'Where are you from?' Liam ask tentatively.

He felt the man blush as he said quietly, 'Africa, Ethiopia.'

'Ah,' Liam smiled, 'Abebe Bikila.'

The man suddenly relaxed and extended his hand.

'How do you do Abebe Bikila!'

Liam shook his head.

'I wish.'

'I'd be an Olympic marathon champion?'

'Ex Africa semper aliquid novi,' the man recited. 'And where are you from, my friend?'

'Ireland, the Republic,' Liam relaxed in the man's company.

'Ah, Joyce and Yeats,' the man replied.

Liam held out his hand.

'Pleased to meet you, Joyce Yeats.'

'Runners and writers,' the man laughed.

'Not bad stereotypes,' Liam agreed.

The waitress intervened and the man ordered. Liam excused himself and they shook hands again.

The curtain moved downstairs as he entered the digs. The room was cold; rain riddled the window. He wasn't conscious of time; had to reclaim the day. The sheets were icy as he drew back the duvet. He was trying to remember when he was an altar boy. Chanting a litany of Latin phrases.

Ex Africa? What did the man in the cafe mean? Liam was drifting off when the meaning dawned on him.

'Always something new from Africa.'

The barefoot Bikila running down the Appian Way in the Rome Olympic marathon certainly was.

Saturday. Cold sunlight and silence. Liam wandered through the day, only aware of token time. Strange faces flitting past on the thronged High Street. Finding the Civil Service office, standing like a sentry on Victoria Street. A cold concrete walk along the seafront, briny and bracing. Lunch at the Lido. Alone.

Returning to the digs he met a black man on the way out. They hesitated before passing politely on the stairs. A tinge of shyness heightened the man's face. 'Ex Africa' came to mind again. He thought for a moment that it might be him. A restless breeze turned the curtain in his room. He watched it like an expectation.

When he went downstairs the landlady confided with clacking teeth.

'I've got a coloured staying, but he won't be eating with my guests.'

Liam felt a surge of shame and answered sharply.

'I know, I met him.'

No blacks.
No Irish.
No dogs.

Bitch, he thought.

There was a lorry driver and a cinema usher staying permanently. They all had dinner at six in a monosyllabic silence. Afterwards Liam sat in the lounge reading 'A Portrait'. The Ritz cinema usher came in reading a comic.

'What are you reading mate?'

'Joyce, A Portrait of the Artist.'

'Of the traitor you mean,' the comic man said coldly.

'No, the Artist as a Young Man,' Liam corrected him.

'Oh, he changed when he grew up then.'

'Very funny,' Liam humoured him.

'Was he always a Lord,' the man waffled on.

'Lord? James Joyce! Not that I know of,' Liam was worn out.

'You'd be too young to remember his broadcasts. Not to mention being from Eire,' he persisted.

'You mean he read from his novels, like Ulysses,' Liam knew he was wasting his breath.

'No, like I said he was a traitor, a Nazi.'

He's not getting it, Liam thought.

'Not that Joyce; I'd say he was apolitical,' Liam was nonplussed.

'A political ponce, more like. Selling his soul to the Nazis,' he wasn't giving up.

'But he lived in Zurich. Neutral,' Liam plugged away.

'Not this Joyce, or Lord Haw as he was called,' he was still getting his wires crossed.

'Well, the Joyce I'm reading wasn't a Lord nor that funny to be called 'Haw'. Twice!'

'Haven't you heard of Finnegan's Wake or Ulysses?' Liam knew the answer to that.

'Yeah, Finnegan's Wake is a racehorse; he died a few times with my money on his back.

Ulysses? wasn't he a general in the American Civil War?'

'Blimey! A Yankee with Finnegan's Wake. Now that's funny, ha, ha,' and he got up to go.

Liam couldn't continue to read after that surreal savaging and settled for the TV. After news at ten he said goodnight to the landlady. She replied 'ta, ta,' as if talking to a child. He moped around his room thinking of home. In bed he imagined Sarah with taut tenderness. White tides surged in the night.

Reading the Sunday newspapers instead of Mass prayers. Outside, middle aged men bathing cars in sickening servitude. No fashion parade up the aisle. Only the casual triviality of Sunday strolls.

Liam felt the day fade along the seafront. Walking past a park: 'Per Mare, Per Ecclesiam'. Fitful football matches. Yellow light at four saw him home. Roast beef and Yorkshire pudding for dinner.

The green covered poems of Hesse, his companion in the opposite chair. Writing home. Wrenching the words out. A destiny of doubt. Writing home to talk to someone. The room moved in around him. Cold. Clicking coins into the gas meter. On the surface of sleep in the heavy fumes. Something his mother used to say came into his mind.

'You're dressing a cold bed for yourself.' In crisp, cruel sheets he drifted in and out of sleep.

After a fitful sleep Liam awoke with a nervous knot in his stomach. He could hardly eat the over fried breakfast the landlady, silently, served him. The office was a short walk up the High Street, towering fifteen stories, on the road out of town. The first day dragged with an induction course. Estuary accents all round him hinting at their London origins. Liam felt like an alien in a new planet, planet Essex. They were finally finished by four after signing the Official Secrets Act. Even the colour of the carpet couldn't be divulged. The conductor of the induction course told them with a knowing smile. His first day and nobody spoke his name.

He felt homesick, missing his parents, Carlo, the collie, even his sister Aine. There was nowhere to sit in the evenings except with the landlady in her lounge. His heart sinking when he heard the dreary theme tune for Coronation Street.

Eventually he settled into the routine of a hectic office. People importantly walking up and down the 'long room,' buff folders clutched under their arms. He was told the trick of looking busy was to have a folder every time you got up from your desk. He got talking to a couple around his own age and they invited him to come for a lunchtime drink. This was the traditional Friday visit to the pub on the London Road. One of them was Mark who would become a lifelong friend. The other one was Fiona, a Scot with a wicket tongue. It was Mark who gave him an application form for the Sports Club.

He was asked was he any good at football. That threw him for a moment thinking it was Gaelic. That answer would have been a 'no.' He told Mark that he played soccer for his University in Ireland.

'Soccer? That's what Americans call football, mate,' Mark was scathing.

After that Liam called it football except when he was in Ireland. Or America if he ever got there! Whatever it was called Liam signed on for the first five-a-side in the Civil Service club pitch.

On the Friday before the first game, they were in the pub as usual when Mark said, 'We'll have to look out for Roger.'

'Why so?' Liam asked.

'Well, haven't you twigged the way he minces down the office?'

'So, he's a bit limp wristed.'

'But he's not the goalie so he won't be playing with his wrist, not in public anyway,' Fiona laughed wickedly.

Liam had to buy a pair of trainers; he didn't want to waste any money on football boots. They were winning one nil at half time, scored by Mark. At the start of the second half Liam was dribbling down the wing when he was upended by the 'chopper' on the other team. The next time 'chopper' got the ball, didn't Roger hammer into him, leaving him squirming on the ground? Mark came over to clap Roger on the back and turned and winked at Liam.

'How wrong were we about limp wristed Roger?' After the game Roger stayed in the dressing room and Liam could see he was too embarrassed to get in the shower.

'Sure, we can have a shower when we get home instead of queuing,' he stayed with Roger.

As he was leaving the clubhouse after a shandy, he realised that he had learned some valuable lessons in his short time in England.

Liam's unit won the tournament outright and he scored a hat trick in the final. After the game they all went for an Indian which scalded the mouth off Liam. Mark gave him the moniker 'Besty,' after his scoring exploits.

'As if, it would be better than pushing pens anyway,' Liam laughed.

'What about yourself?'

'You're very good at running off the ball.'

'I'm usually running away from the ball,' he said modestly.

'Well actually, that's my sport. Running.'

'I compete for the local club, middle-distance.' he explained.

The five a side petered out coming up to Christmas and Mark invited Liam to a track training night at his club. Mark introduced him to Jamie, his training partner. Close cropped hair, gold earring in his left ear, full of chat. What Liam would call a gas man. But he was a fireman actually.

Liam watched them hammer out an interval session, twenty-eight seconds on the button. Liam thought he might give it a try in the New Year; he had done some juvenile cross-country as a schoolboy.

Mark was a serious athlete, often training during his lunch hour. Liam started to run a bit in the park near the track and eventually joined Mark three times a week on his lunch time runs. He could tell that Mark was nursing him along as he let Liam set the pace. Before long Liam would be fit enough to join the club long run every Sunday. Soon he was able to manage a slow ten miler.

Just before Christmas Liam had a letter from his mother with her much younger sister's telephone number and address in London. When he rang her from his landlady's telephone, she invited him to Christmas dinner.

'Didn't want you to be on your lonesome on your first Christmas away from home,' she said.

The Office broke up at lunchtime and he went for a quick jar with Mark and Fiona. At five he packed a duffle bag and caught the Liverpool Street train. He was up and down escalators trying to find the Bakerloo line. It was pitch black when he exited the Underground at Queen's Park. He had to ask in an Indian corner shop for directions. He was relieved when he saw the entrance to the park; Una was opposite the main gate.

A stale smell of frying escaped when Una opened the door. Air was also exhaled from his lungs when she crushed him to her generous bosom. A fair fringed girl of about four clung to her skirts. Her big, blue eyes were poking around her mother's back, trying to get a peek at him.

'Angie, this is your cousin from Ireland. First, mind you,' she winked at Liam.

'The cat's got her tongue,' when there was no response.

In the lounge upstairs, an imitation gas fire glowed like real. Electric candles shone from the window overlooking the park.

'I see you're keeping up the old traditions,' Liam looked out over the park

'More modern now, no more wax although I miss that Christmassy smell,' she took his bag.

'Sit yourself down while I put this in your room.'

In an alcove leading to the kitchen a Christmas tree sparkled, presents wrapped at the base. Una came back via the kitchen with a pot of tea on a tray.

'Angie, would you fetch the biscuits, there's a good girl.'

When Angela came back with a plate of coconut creams Una told her to give them to Liam.

'Only one, so,' he smiled and handed the plate back.

'You can have the rest.'

Her shyness had dissipated.

'Mum, you can have one too as well.'

'Thanks. Generosity is her middle name,' Una cuffed her curls.

Timmie, her husband was down in Harlesden buying Christmas drinks for his men. Liam thought he might have met him once when they were home on holiday. A subbie from Connemara singing 'Galway Bay' in the Corner House. When he returned Angela flew down the stairs when she heard his key in the lock.

'Daddy's girl,' Una raised her eyebrows.

After a chicken casserole and a glass of wine Una asked Liam if he wanted to go to Midnight Mass with them. His mother must have alerted her; it was a long time since he went. He walked the short distance; Midnight Mass was different. Nostalgic. The familiar carols before the bell; Adeste Fideles. He still remembered the Latin words from his boyhood in the choir.

A wave of homesickness swept over him. His mind was returning, wandering back in the music. It was the singing of 'Silent Night' that took him back, home again.

A black frost fell early on Christmas Eve. It was melted on the lane when Liam got up. His father had to brave it in the dark morning. He was bringing fodder to the Upper Meadow for the animals. By the time Liam had pulled on his short trousers, his father was coming out of the cowhouse. Daisy had given a good sup into the enamel bucket, but the cranky cow had reneged.

The keen cold held solid all day. It was the last night out in the Carols. Liam's voice hadn't broken yet, so he was to the front with the sopranos. A secondary teacher led the choir, boys and girls. The nuns weren't allowed out in the world. 'Silent Night' ascended into the cold and crowded night sky. Afterwards they all had red lemonade and Kimberley biscuits in the Monastery.

Later the choir would form again for Midnight Mass. At half eleven they trooped up the stairs by the Tower door. The church was half empty, nobody keeping vigil before the crib. Liam prayed to the Eternal Infant in the silence. When the church filled up the organist began to play 'Adeste Fideles'. The sacred sadness of the Latin carol descended over the people below. 'Venite, venite in Bethlehem.' Into the village by the side of a hill, stretching white with drifts of silence to the cold sky.

The bell for Mass sounded and the choir was on its feet. Liam felt happy; a new peace, a growing peace settled over him. He would treasure that night when other nights blew black and bitter.

They all filed down the stairs for Communion. The white host was cool on his tongue. He walked slowly back up the stairs, alone but for the body of Christ. He closed his eyes and said the prayers after holy Communion in his mind. He watched the three aisles of people shuffling to the altar rails, hungry for the bread of life. He was sad when the last blessing was made. It was over, he walked out into the iced air.

The snow had stopped falling, on the streets the first coat lay. He crunched home, carefully, leaving his imprint on the night. His mother was frying Denny's sausages. He had a feed with his father and went to bed full to the brim.

A light fall of snow resumed on Christmas morning and he was happy to watch the world turn white. The fire was blazing in the range; his mother was baking Christmas cakes. A rich currant and a golden madeira. Everything smelled sweet and warm, pure and white. Christmas day.

His father minded the animals, even on Christmas day he had to work. Liam drew on his Wellingtons and helped with the feed. He struggled to draw a bale of hay to the Upper Meadow. He milked Daisy, the quiet cow and left the cranky cow to his father who had to spancel her. When they had finished their chores, they washed and were ready for the feast.

The table was set for four, once Aine made an appearance. She needed her beauty sleep; nobody disagreed with her. Feisty was the word if you could get it in edgeways. She wore nylons for the first time, seams crooked in a pair of high heels. She called them stilettos.

'Sounds dangerous,' his father said drolly.

A child dressed up as a woman.

The red candle in the middle of the table. Round shadows from the balloons on the walls. The decorations dimmed the light as they triangled across the ceiling. The kettle sung on the range. Cold turkey for tea. Cutting the current cake for a late supper. Mikado, Kimberley and Custard Cream biscuits with red lemonade. We were worn out from eating. Christmas night.

His father was drinking a bottle of stout and Liam turned up his nose when he was offered a sup. Drinking red lemonade instead while Aine had a Wonder Orange. That figures he thought; it would hardly be ordinary orange. When his mother had her annual glass of sherry Aine took a sip and convulsed in coughing.

His father told tales of olden times; some tall like the night he saw the Pooka. Laughing at the hard times of his youth. Going back to the places where he left his boyhood. Walking in his bare feet across a slough on a frosty morning to get to school. A square of bread called caudy and a bottle of milk to see him through the day. His own father evicted from his tenant farm, like his father before him. By the land agent of Lord Lansdowne. Sheltering his family by a ditch until he could pay the rent. The rugby crowd called their stadium after the Lord. Lansdowne Road.

After another bottle of stout his father started to hum. Liam asked him to give them a few bars in a man-to-man voice. He sang 'Oft in the Stilly Night,' his voice young and clear. His mind still turning back the years. He told them about the singsongs in his own father's house. The all-night wedding dances that ended in the dawn. Music and dancing at the cross-roads of a summer's evening. Liam could imagine the waning sun catching the pale blue of his eyes. Only his hair was lost now. Lost like his boyhood forever.

Aine was coaxed into a song and she sang 'Wooden Heart' which had his father raising his eyes. 'Elvis Presley sings it,' she explained afterwards.

'Who is he while he's at home?' Liam's mother asked.

'A rock and roll singer,' Aine exclaimed, her eyes coming to life.

'Does he now, rock and roll too?' his father teased.

A few more songs and stories and the night gave way. The fire in the range was let die down. The empty bottles put in a crate under the stairs. Liam's mother lit the four candles to place in the windows. To shine throughout the night, showing the way. A scrap of poetry came into his head.

A Summer:

'Things bright and green, things young and happy.'

His father's:

'Will pass and change, will die and be no more.'

Liam went up the stairs thinking those very thoughts would be his memories too. He looked out the window of the bathroom. It was pitch black; he couldn't see the river. But all down the valley candles shone in windows. He lay awake watching the candlelight play on the ceiling, smelling the melting wax. Tired out, he drifted to sleep with the image of his father's fair hair, dancing at the crossroads of a summer's evening. The declining sun catching the pale blue of his eyes. Only his hair was lost now. Lost like Liam's boyhood, forever.

'And I have gone upon my way
Sorrowful.'

When Mass ended Liam found himself shaking hands with strangers; people that Una and Timmie seemed to know. A multi-cultural mix of Irish, African, English and Caribbean. In the clear, crisp early morning they walked back to Queens Park. Angie was agitated in anticipation of Santa and went straight to bed. Una cooked a ream of Donnelly's sausages and bacon and it was getting on for two when the house settled down.

Christmas day dawned dull and drizzly. Liam slipped out in his tracksuit for a five-mile run around Queens Park, the cool air clearing his head. Una had a plate of sausage rolls and a mug of coffee ready for him after his shower. Timmie was going back to his local, the Harp, in Harlesden and Liam was invited too.

When they opened the door the rough and raucous bar was rocking. Most of Timmie's gang were mountainy men from Connemara. They were shipping pints and whiskey chasers. Liam felt out of it, as if from a different tribe. He heard a couple of men speaking Irish which didn't help. He overheard a throwaway comment about 'a posh Paddy,' and he took it to mean him. It could be the glass of wine he was drinking as he knew that's what they'd be having for dinner. He didn't believe in mixing the grape and grain. He had nursed two glasses in the couple of hours they were there.

Before the massive Christmas dinner, he gave Una a bottle of Chanel no. 5 and Timmie a bottle of Old Spice. Angie was delighted with her rag doll he'd found in Woolworths. In return he was given an Adidas top and the inevitable socks.

After dinner Angie pulled him out of his chair and he found himself stretched on the carpet. Santa had dropped her a My Little Pony down the chimney. She had Liam galloping along the floor for the afternoon. After the Queen's message, which Timmie objected to, they all dozed off in the warmth of the room.

On Saint Stephen's Day - or Boxing Day in the native vernacular - Timmie went to the local bookies. He had got a pub tip for the King George which proved expensive. Liam took the chance to get a long run in down at Wormwood Scrubs. The cold air and the exercise the best cure he knew for a hangover.

The Christmas holiday passed quickly and next day he said his goodbyes. He had to promise Angie he'd be back next year for another race with 'My Little Pony' as she gave him her 'big hug'. Una packed a doggie bag for the journey home. If only he had Carlo! More turkey. Cold.

January was a dreary month for training, long and bleak. Liam had to force himself out in the cold, dark nights after work. Sometimes if he had done a lunchtime run, he'd leave it. He found it fatal to sit down for a cup of tea. So, he got into the habit of pulling on his gear the minute he got back to the digs. He slogged the miles on his own until the long run, mainly with Mark. Jamie was on shift work with the Brigade, as he called it. On Sundays it was steady state running for ten miles. The time flying along with their pace. Chatting about the previous day's football. From Man U to Millwall. Mark said it was from 'the sublime to the surreal.' Liam wasn't sure which was which.

They called Sunday night their down time with eighty to a hundred miles in the 'bank'. The White Horse became their local as it was equal distance between them. Jamie joined them occasionally, usually with a blonde in tow. They were fascinated with his gold earring, never having seen a man wear one before. Mark was musing on why only one. He reckoned he wore it on the left to go with his politics. Liam would see him from his office window, outside Victoria station, selling the Morning Star. The only time he made a sale would be because of the blonde by his side.

Their limit was a round each but with Jamie there would have to be 'one for the roadwork,' his little joke. At around eight o'clock the landlord's son emerged shyly from behind the bar. A tousled haired boy around Angie's age standing before the jukebox. When the landlord put in the coins the little boy started to dance, always to the Birdie song.

After a while they got to know some of the regulars. Especially a man they came to know as Derek the Dust. He'd come over to their table when The Crystal Chandelier was played and tried to get them to join in. Liam didn't mind the cheesy song, but Mark was a bit of a rocker and Jamie couldn't abide it.

'Bet Charlie Pride is worried,' he muttered as Derek was murdering the music.

Spring was a great time to be an athlete. The foundation had been laid, the sharpening up beginning. Eyeballs out intervals on cold Tuesday nights on the cinder track. Road relays of 5k all over Essex. The track season imminent. Mark upping the ante hoping for a sub four 1500 m. Liam desperately trying to stay with Mark on the 200m with 40 seconds recovery. Running along the Golden Mile in the Spring, evenings inexorably stretching out. As the months went by it became a game of weaving in and out between the day-trippers, mainly from London.

The boats on the Estuary were listing lazily as Liam stepped up his training along the Esplanade. In the summer, the seafront was packed with people. The smell of fast-food vying with the briny sea breeze. Wine and vinegar in the air. Bingo callers battling with dalek voiced fruit machines. Tacky topless pubs where beer and blood flowed on weekends. Coaches of London cousins smashing smiles from Saturday night faces. Feeling alien and exiled in a cultural wasteland.

The inanity of office life relieved by a new girl starting. Liam was charged with showing her the repetitive routine. Older women eying her brazen blonde hair. The triumphant thrust of her breasts as she sashayed down the office. Watching her tight buttocks spread as she bent over a filing cabinet. Liam's eyes also lingered and longed as she tantalised. Because he didn't have a girlfriend there were hints that he was a 'homo'. Not quite sapiens! Only wimps would wait; be faithful to a fantasy.

The desperation of digs, the emptiness of weekends. In the absence of Sarah, it was Roxy who filled in the void in his life.

Mark had given him a schedule for the 1500m in the Civil Service championship. Long runs and reps, fartlek and tempo runs. And Mark's speciality 200m with 40 second recovery. After a month of diligent training Liam was peaking for the meeting in Crystal Palace. Mark would be targeting another sub four 1500m in Birmingham the same time.

Liam felt the tension of the race increase when he saw Roxy board the office coach. The brilliant boldness of her eyes pierced as she passed down the aisle. Crystal Palace was sparse with spectators when the coach arrived. Roxy wished him 'good luck' as he jumped off, her lips glistening in the heat.

The ritual routine of the warm-up took 40 minutes. Jogging, stretching and striding. Adrenalin drying the mouth, the sun drawing a drench of sweat to the forehead. Alone in a mantra before the sacrifice.

The gun released him from his fetters of fear. He forgot the tingling tension in his stomach. The first lap flew by, jockeying for position. He was floating on the footsteps of the leader into the second lap. When it began to hurt on the third lap his eyed glazed over. Lactic loaded down his legs as they took the bell. He felt the faint glint of gold on the crown of the top bend, surging to the leader's shoulder. At 300m he kicked for home. A decisive spurt of speed at 200m and he hit the home straight. The sun travelling off the tartan to blind him. Anaerobic agony leading him into oxygen debt. Eyeballs out as he hit the tape. Giddy as a new-born foal at the line. Hands on his knees as the rasp of breath slowly subsided.

After a long cool down he headed for the showers. When he emerged, the relays were concluding the meeting. The presentation was held in the shadow of the stand on the home straight.

Liam felt Roxy's eyes watchful, as he jumped on the podium. The evening sun scattered thin shadows across the grass arena. People drifted away to the beer tent, others to the disco. Liam gathered his gear and wrapped his spikes in his damp towel. At the bar he hurled a Heineken down his parched throat. He queued at the food bar for a cheeseburger to go with his second pint. He could hear the disco getting going in a hall next door. Office cliques clung together in groups. Smoke curled around his head, invading his eyes. The residue of the race and the beer made him feel tired. He forced his legs to keep time with the music.

Liam watched a gang of girls from the office dancing. White stilettos around a circle of handbags. 'Sharon and Tracey's'. He leaned on the bar a pint foaming in his hand. He wished Mark were here; but he was far away in Birmingham running in a British miler's race. Much too good for this standard, Liam thought. He saw Roxy at the other end of the bar ordering a tray of drinks. The dancing girls sat down at a table when she returned with their drinks. Later he glimpsed her on the crowded dancefloor. A tight white top clung to her breasts, a flash of flesh in the vee. A pair of blue Levi's blended taut to her buttocks. Mesmerised by the movement, the music, the leaping lights, he felt lightheaded. He lost sight of her in the crowd lurching to the bar. After another pint he saw her part the huddle near his end of the bar.

'Aren't ye dancing,' she glanced up.

'Well, not with myself anyway,' he felt himself redden.

A film of sweat settled on her upper lip. He could smell the faint smell of perfume.

'Are ye askin,' she smiled archly.

'I can jog but I can't jive,' he tried to joke.

'I can teach you in a tick tonight,' she nodded to the heaving floor.

'It'll take more than one night,' he hinted nervously.

'But ye're supposed to be fit,' she pursued.

'Well...' he trailed off.

'Well, well ye're a star. So, shine tonight,' she commanded.

'I did today,' he said modestly. 'I don't come out at night,' his voice was droll.

She slapped his arm and they both laughed. The initial air of tension subsided. As she ordered the drinks, she spoke out of the corner of her mouth.

'What's your poison.'

'Had enough, thanks.'

Her hair shaded her face like a shield as she turned.

'Ye really should go out more often,'

'Who'd take me?'

'Any girl would.'

'You'd better show me the steps so,' his mouth was dry.

'Righto, ye're on. I shall return, be prepared,' she flashed a smile over her shoulder.

Liam drained his glass of warm beer. He felt hemmed in by the heaving crowd. Not unlike being boxed in during a race, he thought. Roxy was slowly edging through the throng. He saw her face flush in a strobe light.

Sarah's face surfaced briefly. He felt his life was about to take a new turn. Reality reached with the hot hand that grasped his palm. Lactic acid still hung heavy in his muscles after the race. Roxy was like a marionette on a string, a doll in a dance. Her face blurred in the dimming light. A half smile forming on her face, oval, avid. A medley of Stones was blasting out. Roxy's lips were fumbling with the words.

'I canna get no satisfaction.'

Teasing and tantalising his tense senses. When the music changed to 'Wonderful Tonight,' she rested a hand on his shoulder. Old fashioned, he placed one arm round her waist and grasped her hand at his shoulder. She guided his hand to the one at her waist. Her arms grasped his neck, fondling his hair. The ridge of her buttocks swelled in his hands.

He could feel the taut touch of her breasts. Incongruously, it was he who melted in her arms. He realised he had never danced like this before. After the sequence they found a pair of barstools. Roxy went back to her table while he bought her a vodka and lime. When he returned from the bar the group of girls were staring over. Roxy waved a dismissive hand to the girls and sashayed across the dancefloor.

It was strange that they only had one dance. As if it was a ritual that enabled them to touch. Now they were sipping silently and holding hands. Filling in the emptiness of the night. Fondling fate, intent on a journey. The noise around them intensified as the drink flowed. They sat together watching the inebriated, in the ritual dance of a different tribe.

On the coach home Roxy left her head linger on his shoulder. He smelled the smoke snaking through her hair. He was conscious of her closeness, coaxing, kindling.

On a tide of anticipation, he closed his eyes and drifted in a dream. Liam had put in for a flexi-day to recover from the race. The long weekend like a sentence before him. Words were forming in his mind...

'Would you like to?'

'Pictures, pub...'

Roxy was murmuring musically in his ear.

'Would ye like to go to the beach, tomorrow?'
Her eyes danced dangerously as she added.
'Picnic on the pebbles.'

There was as much shingle as sand on the ten-mile seafront. Not so long ago he would have said Roxy was forward. There would be no fantasy this time. The shrapnel of Ireland would wound. A figment of Israel would fade. Fragments of flesh would adorn the future.

They had arranged to meet at the White Horse. Liam had a lie-in, the ache of the race still in his legs. The landlady was livid; she had a cooked breakfast ready at nine. When he surfaced at ten, she ignored him. He said 'good boy' to the dog. She was fussing over her fawn Labrador, on speaking terms with him. The dog was simpering and slobbering over her jowls.

'Walkies, walkies,' she repeated as the door slammed.

The large dog took her for its walk and Liam left for the Lido for a late breakfast. Thinking of Roxy, he decided to give notice. He would try to find a flat, declare independence. Invite Roxy and who knows?

Black leggings and a tan tee shirt. Roxy was waiting at the traffic lights fending off some adolescent whistles. A scut of skinheads were loitering and laughing outside the pub. Roxy looked different in daylight. Her hair shone with lacquer; a breeze brushed fair strands across her face. The glint had faded from her eyes. She smiled slowly, almost demurely. The youths scattered towards the seafront as Liam approached.

'Was that the species Yobus Britanicus,' Liam dismissed the louts.

Roxy laughed, unsure of the pidgin Latin.

'Ye're not including the Scousers, are ye?'

Liam raised his hands, 'Au contraire,' he apologised.

'Bloody Betsy, when did you become bi-lingual?' she linked his arm.

'Overnight, since I met you.'

'Besides, Liverpool is the second capital of Ireland.'

'Same tribe then I suppose,' she said doubtfully.

They laughed and moved closer as they made for the seafront.

The mid-day sun scorched the grass in Southchurch Park. A haze hung above the cinder track, raising the dust. Liam imagined moments of pain in training before the glory of gold. Why do we do it? he wondered. But he knew why; it made us feel alive. The length of the front was sagging with people. A pubescent parade of girls in bikinis passed across the stony sand. Roxy glanced at him, archly. Liam pretended his eyes were elsewhere, gazing grandly over the Estuary to the coast of Kent. Roxy carried a basket of beer and sandwiches and Liam took one handle. Together, they wandered along the Esplanade looking for a space. Liam was struck by the iconoclasm of her clothes as he had to walk behind her, letting the basket go.

Black and tan: the cruel colour of history. He remembered his Grandmother telling of the terror visited on small farms.

'Like hounds in a hunt; baying in strange accents for blood,' she used to say, as if it was yesterday.

Bullets fired for fun towards remote farmhouses nestling in the comfort of the hills. Over her daughter's eight-year-old head, his mother. Way beyond her innocence.

Liam thought of her then when she was alive, a tall figure in a black skirt and shawl. With hairpins twinkling in her hair, which was the style of her generation. He must have been the same age too, eight, when she had a fall on the farm. Shortly after his mother told him 'your Nan's gone to heaven.'

He was led into the dead room by his father. The room was hushed, with a Christmas smell by the candlelight glowing on her face. The bed looked pallid with her face soft against the brown habit. Hands cold in prayer, fingers entwined in her black rosary beads. Her hard life over and left holding hands only with herself.

'Wakey, wakey,' Roxy removed him from his reverie.

'Sorry, miles away,' he was contrite.

'Miles!'

'You're not still running?'

'Only round my head.'

Hidden from history Roxy carried her colours proudly. They were passing balconies overlooking the Estuary, framed by walled gardens. Roads revealing familiar names through glinting trees. Tyrone Road, Antrim Road in Essex?

The heat intensified; the sweat simmered on Liam's forehead. Roxy found a sheltered patch of sand. Spreading a couple of bath towels, they flung themselves down. They gazed out over a horizon of haze on the water. A heavy woman was swimming out from the shore, her putrid pink flesh wobbling on the waves. After eating, Liam stretched out his heavy legs. Roxy fingered her hair back from her brow. As she lay back Liam could see the outline of her breasts jutting to the sky.

Roxy startled him as she pulled the ring from a beer can. She licked the fizzy head before handing the warm amber liquid to him. Liam scanned the distance where the Isle of Grain scattered along the Kent coast. On the foreshore yachts were listing on the glazed water. Roxy's hand was electric on his arm.

'Come on, let's have a paddle at least,' she jumped up.

'I knew I should have brought my bikini,' Liam shed his trainers.

'Ye haven't the chest for it, dearie,' she hauled him to the water.

'At least one of us has,' he laughed as she bobbed up and down a wave.

'Aye, they run in the family. In pairs,' she smiled.

As Liam followed her to the edge of the water he knew. From now on he would also be running in pairs.

And that hot Saturday night they paired up for the first time. Meeting in the Papillon, near her seafront flat. Roxy was drinking vodka and orange and Liam reverted to lager and lime. The obese barman was talking to another customer. He heard him say 'that's a terrible way to drink lager.' But he paused for effect, 'but a great way to drink lime.' They were laughing loudly as Liam left the bar with his order. 'Essex eejits' Liam was thinking setting down the drinks.

Roxy was wearing a pencil slim skirt and a white top; the word 'Kop' written across her breasts. The contrast between the black and white setting off the day's tan. Liam noticed her eyes roving around the bar as they shared office gossip. In a stilted silence they finished their drinks. When Roxy got her round in, she was at the bar for a long time, chatting to the two at the bar. There was no lime in Liam's pint; he let it go without comment.

Roxy wanted an Indian take-away when they finished the second drink. The two at the bar were ogling her as they left; she knew but didn't let on.

A curry in this heat he was thinking as they walked back into the High Street. Roxy did the ordering; Chicken Tikka Masala and Onion Bhaji. They bought a bottle of wine, Jacobs Creek in an offie on the way back to Roxy's flat. She was sharing with Fiona, a Scot and Roxy, a scouser. They took a shortcut through Southchurch Hall Park. Near the duck pond Roxy slipped her free hand into his with a coy smile. Was she tipsy, he wondered as she gave his hand a quick squeeze.

They ate in the kitchen and took the coffees to the sofa, in the lounge. Afterwards, Roxy snuggled up to him a hand resting, casually, on his thigh. He could feel the heat from her sun warmed body. He could taste the spicy food on her breath.

When she raised her lips, her tongue flicked his teeth and wrapped around his. His hand ran over the 'Kop' motif between her breasts. He dropped his other hand to the top of her skirt, sliding between her tanned thighs. He hesitated because he didn't have protection. His hands were redundant when she slid to the carpet. Unzipping his jeans, she licked him through his boxers. Pulling them down she took him in her mouth. He was thrusting against her tongue until he was spent.

'Bloody hell, as the locals say.' He exhaled as she sat back on the sofa.

'Ye mean, bloody good,' she said tartly.

'That too, thanks,' and he drew her close.

After that he could only see her on Saturday nights. That was a pattern that went on during the track season. Racing most weekends and travelling all over the Southern Counties every fortnight. Liam knew it wasn't enough for Roxy. He had to say no to pints and parties. Then one sunny Sunday in the White Horse, Mark spotted her on her own, in an alcove. Liam was at the bar chatting to Derek the Dust while waiting to be served. When he got the pints in Mark whispered, 'in the corner.' As Liam, discreetly, glanced over Roxy was rising from her seat. She had her arms out as a tall, stocky man came through the door. They embraced, briefly, and disappeared into the alcove.

Jamie was raising a toast to Mark; he had broken the four-minute barrier for the 1500m. Liam clinked the two glasses; it was over with Roxy. They had helped the club win the league match beating Windsor, Slough and Eton on their track.

'How posh was that?' Jamie was joking.

'A triple barrel name?'

'That's what I call winning the class war,' he couldn't let politics out of it.

'Bleedin ell' Jamie, it was just a race. Maybe a bit of a battle but hardly a war,' Mark was as modest as ever.

Liam was thinking it was far from Eton we were educated. After a raucous rendition of 'The Crystal Chandelier' they left, with Jamie cringing as usual.

Passing the car park Mark noticed some movement in the back seat of a car. Jamie was saying 'look at that.'

'A bird with her assets in the air.' Roxy?

'She was going down in the forest there,' Jamie was telling us.

'What do you mean,' Mark was puzzled.

'You know, looking for wood,' licking the sap,' Jamie had a way with words.

'Jamie, you're a metaphor for misogyny,' Mark chided him.

'Me? I don't even know Miss Ogyny,'

'I wouldn't mind with her though,' he added.

Mark gave up then and they parted for the night. Eventful.

Liam was almost relaxed, the relationship with Roxy was petering out. He made one final phone call to her. He told her he saw her at the White Horse, and she admitted she was going out with a local footballer. He said they were there to celebrate Mark breaking four minutes for the 1500m.

'Well done him,' she said. 'So that's your life. Only running?'

Taken aback he replied sharply.

'Not really, but it's my passion,' adding 'what's yours?'

'Nookie,' she said.

'That figures,' he laughed.

After that they hung up and called it a day.

The season was petering out; only a 10k road race in Southend and an open meeting in London in September. Liam, Mark and Jamie all ran their last race together; the classic 10k along the seafront. The pressure was on Mark to defend his home patch. He had just won his first British vest in Paris, coming second in a fast 3k. This was a sharpener for the 5k Classic and he bounded up Pier Hill to establish an early lead. Five runners went sub thirty in a breezy autumnal morning with Mark leading the way. Jamie posted a personal best while Liam had a casual one, coming home in his own good time.

Later, in the White Horse Mark told them he had met a national coach in Paris. So, his schedule was about to change but he would still do the long runs on Sundays with us. Up to then Mark was self-coached devouring training manuals and athletic magazines. It was a feature in Athletics Monthly that he saw an invitation to train in Israel. He would have to work on a kibbutz for six hours a day for food and accommodation.

Israel didn't go down too well with Jamie which came as no surprise. Jamie was a strong advocate of the Palestinian cause and likewise Liam but more nuanced. Like Ireland the two-state solution to a colonial conundrum. After a mild debate Mark and Jamie came to a compromise; they agreed not to mix sport and politics. Liam 's contribution was: 'as if it was that simple.' They all shook hands at the end and Jamie would not race again but would do his winter training with Liam.

'I remember certain mornings between spring and summer, after the long runs in the woods, after the winter training, when I experienced an extraordinary feeling of completeness... an exaltation. I burned with impatience to throw myself into the battles of the home straight. They would say to me: it's peak form. I know now that it has another name – le bonheur. You have never been truly young if you have not known such moments. But one day the time comes when your best form will never return and on rather a sad note you leave the games of your youth forever. Yet you have achieved some fulfilment. Sport teaches us to love life passionately and to accept it as it is without cheating.'

Michel Clare

When the evenings began to draw in Liam got that feeling. The dread of darkness. Steeling his mind to face another winter's raining. Imagining relentless rains as he warmed up in the soft September sun. He could feel the sweat oozing from his forehead as he flicked his legs at the end of a stride. The crispness wasn't there. The last race of a long season. He felt adrenalin dry, heavy legs and heavier heart.

The sharp crack of the starting gun made him pause. The 1500m field were away. He watched the initial burst down the back straight. The aristocrats of running. He felt a pang of nostalgia. It was once his event in the seasons of his prime. When the speed was in his legs; he could change gear in a couple of strides.

He heard the timekeeper shout out the lap times 55,56,57... He gave Mark a shout; they had travelled up to the Palace together. Mark had sent off the entries and persuaded Liam into a 10k. It was an open meeting and the standard stretched like the field in the second lap. Four had broken away by the third lap with Mark tucked in at the leader's shoulder. He looked comfortable with that effortless, bouncing style.

The sinking sun sliced through the four figures as they took the bell. The red vest Mark was wearing flamed for an instant, fusing with the fire in his face. Liam gave him another shout, seeing the suffering on the face of the leader. Mark seemed to incline his head, then he was off on an extended kick. The surprise move at 250m opened a short gap but the other three quickly recovered. Liam felt a slight twinge of adrenaline for Mark as he hit the home straight. The gap squeezed as he began to tie up, but he pumped his arms to carry his legs through the tape. The winner.

The next race was the 10k and Liam jogged across to the start. Mark was just lifting his head; there was a glazed look in his eyes. Liam knew the feeling well: the whirling head, the rapid rasp in the throat and the lactic in the legs. But the flying feeling as you kicked for home was worth all the puny pain in the end.

'Great run Mark,' Liam was sitting down to put on his spikes.

'Thanks mate.'

'It was bloody hard work.'

'I know, knew rather,' Liam was getting to his feet.

'Go on, you've still got it old boy,' Mark started his cool down.

Liam was laughing at the 'old boy'.

'Have a good one,' Mark called over his shoulder.

Liam had time for three strides before the red coated starter called the runners to the line. It was a big field, and he found a place well away from the inside lane.

'On your marks'...the gun raised the runners from their crouches. Meditation in motion. After a desperate lunge for the bend the field settled down to a relaxed rhythm. Liam dropped off the pace and switched off. Steady state running for 25 laps. Concentration became crucial as the laps peeled away. He tried not to notice the lap markers as they came around each time. Years of conditioning made him divide the distance into miles. Feeling free and fluid after a mile. Digging in at two miles as the pace quickened. Surge upon surge down the back straight with the slight breeze. The field finally falling away in total disintegration.

At 5k that sinking feeling that you had to do it all again. Only twice as hard. Running into oxygen debt, your legs going lazy with lactic. The purifying pain that raises the runner above automatons. 'Christ, the bloody agony!' Another burst down the back straight. The leader trying to break away. Stay with it. Lungs labouring. Legs dying under him. He could feel the stinging sweat rolling down his cheeks like bitter tears. A haze before his eyes as they finish another lap. Was that eight? Can't go through it again. The pain barrier is the figment of a masochist imagination? Must be six. He wiped away the sweat with the back of his right hand. Another miserable mile. Then a lousy lap...and... the bell. Another savage surge. The remainder of the field cracks. Only three through the figment; the trailing pack pale fragments in the setting sun.

Going down...gold, silver and bronze. Cold concentration on the two front runners. Every metre mattered now. The pace seemed to settle into a tactical tempo. Waiting for the last lap? Liam forged to the front on the home straight. Token try. The bell. The catalyst setting up the supreme sacrifice. Like a pageant of pain, the three runners carried the colours and cross of the crowd. Sharing pride and pain 300m from calvary.

Shadows shortening around the arena. A freshening breeze across the brow. Liam held the lead at 200m, feeling a fleeting elation. They were on his shoulder. Poised... he couldn't lift his knees as they pushed past, engaged in their own private battle.

Off the last bend...they were gone, into gold and silver. Liam tried again down the home straight. Leaden legs driven by iron will. It wasn't there. Either the legs or the will had wilted. The finishing line. Home.

Calvary conquered. Leaning over the steeplechase barrier. Feeling sick, faint, sad. The tragic trinity. Someone put a palm in his hand.

'Well run.'

Palm. Peace. He shook the hand, weakly. The winners.

His legs wobbled when he tried to walk again. The sweat was cold in the small of his back. Mark came over and handed him his tracksuit.

'You really took them on in the last lap Liam.'

'Well, truth to tell, I was tying up at the bell,' Liam admitted.

'Your reserves must be well in the black then.'

We were interrupted by the results being announced. Name and time flashed on to the giant scoreboard. Bright bronze. Fading light flung from the imminent night sky. Mark cooled down with him even though he'd already jogged a mile. Liam felt the lactic lighten in his legs as they finished. A quick shower and they were on the road. Liam relaxed while Mark took the wheel. Talking of training and times. Mileage and memories.

In a couple of weeks Mark would be off to Israel. The simple socialist alternative to the American scholarship system. The invite in Athletics Monthly eventually prompted him. To work six hours a day and to train in the sunlit citrus groves. Imagine. Idyllic days in December working on the land, the holy land. Lapped by the Sea of Galilee. Soft breezes from Mount Tabor, fanning your face as you ran.

Liam knew he was in the evening of his athletic life. Maybe one more Everest to climb. The marathon? The mountain in his mind.

Later Liam was idly reading Athletics Monthly when he saw an ad for the Israeli national marathon. He and Jamie had upped their mileage after a couple of weeks of active rest.

'The outstanding event of the Israeli athletic calendar is the Sea of Galilee International Marathon'. To take place around the holy and historic lake on December 20th.

He realized Israel wasn't alien. Outside of Ireland it was the first land in his living memory. Wasn't Jerusalem the city state he was searching for in the agony of exile? The ephemeral peace he almost touched in his teens. In the long walks through a little Kerry town. Enclosed in a verdant valley. The Summer sun laid to rest. A scattered reflection on the river. Shadows fading from the hills. Across the lonely lane to the water where his father perished. A silence falling over the night.

It was past midnight when they got home both tired and troubled with their own thoughts. On the second Saturday in October Mark flew to Tel Aviv. They went for a pint with a few of the middle-distance squad before he left. Liam felt a certain sadness as he said goodbye to his training pal. Although it was over six years since the Yom Kippur war the Middle East was still ravelled in a colonial contradiction.

In November Liam and Jamie started the twenty-mile-long runs, the foundation of marathon training. The first ten miles through the sleepy little village of Wakering. Their breaths condensing the crisp air as the miles were knocked out. At fifteen miles the tingling in the thighs as the distance told. The last five miles with legs like lead; dead to the world for the duration. Afternoons, slumped before the TV, drinking litres of orange juice.

Staying in most weekends now; waiting for a letter from Mark. Friday evenings at the laundrette with the week's running gear. Shopping at the Co-Op on Saturdays; occasional pint with Jamie when he was free. Sometimes feeling restless and lonely in the weekend crowds in the High Street.

Out of this mood Liam began to dabble in writing. Doggerel poetry to begin with and then an attempt at a short story. During a mid-week ten miler he got the start of his first vignette. It was a skinning cold night; he pushed the pace from the start to get warm. After five miles his mind was floating halfway between the hills of Galilee and the hill of home. He stole a Christmas scene from his childhood. Buried deep to build a personal pyre to his father. A reflection of his light. A guilt offering that he didn't believe in his everlasting life.

One Saturday he ran into Yussuf in the library. He was a history teacher; the man he met on the stairs of the digs when he first arrived in this town. Liam had picked out four books on the Middle East. Over a coffee in the cafe Liam told Yussuf he was going to Israel.

'Liam my friend, Israel is a reality even for an Arab history teacher.' Go by all means, but with your mind and eyes open. You're ready to suffer for your marathon race.'

'But think as you run: is your pain anything compared to the agony of the Palestinians,' Yussuf ended, his serious brown eyes troubled.

Liam didn't respond for a moment while he drained his coffee.

'Of course, I'll try to understand. You know where I come from, Yussuf.'

'Palestine is people as well as land.'

'Subject to suffering, without a home, scarcely a hope.'

'But Yussuf, you dreamed yourself free in Egypt.' I remember you once told instead of being a teacher you could be a shepherd on the banks of the Nile. Personally, I think it would be more meaningful than teaching history to imperial amnesiacs!' Liam finished jokingly.

'Seriously, I believe that the Palestinians will have their own state someday.'

'In the meantime, I feel I can learn more by travelling, to understand more.'

'As-salamu alaykum, Liam, peace be upon thee,' Yussuf gave him his blessing.

As they parted Liam said he'd send him a postcard from' Palestine.'

Yussuf laughed and held out his hand.

After an early afternoon five miles Liam settled down to read. Green March, Black September; the story of the Palestinian Arabs. He became so engrossed that he missed Man U on match of the day.

'Write down,

I am an Arab,

I am a name without a title,

Steadfast in a frenzied world,

My roots sink deep,

Beyond the ages,

Beyond time.

He lay awake a long time; the night turned, and his mind found succour in sleep. Next morning, he started his last long run on his own. Going through the first ten miles in a grey mist with a cold wind against him. He tried to keep the rhythm going along the seafront, the wind wild in his hair. He vowed to visit the barber as another gust nearly took him off his feet. The last three miles dragged and the little incline on the Boulevard became as hard as a hill. Once he cleared the last summit his mind drifted to the shores of Galilee.

The elation of the run lingered into Monday. A weak winter sun glinted on the grass in Priory Park. A green prism showed through a film of frost. He seemed to flow over a forest. His mind cleared away the offal of the office. The naked trees trembling in a shadow. A cooling cloud across his wet brow. Into the sun for a second lap. Frozen faces filing from a tower block. Turning collars and noses up. He floats across their path, beyond the life of concrete creatures. The grass softens under his feet and he finds himself in its silence. He faintly hears his breathing, feels his footsteps. Mind and body suspended. One. Time better spent in pubs and clubs. Disco here and disco there. Disco nowhere. The moment when running is simply a sacrifice. As close to the sacred silence of the soul as he could ever get.

After those five miles in the forest of his dreams the week was denuded of daylight. By Saturday he could write a hundred miles for the week in his training diary. And his mind was ready for the marathon.

Christmas crowds rushing in and out of shops. Tarnished tinsel on a Christmas tree growing out of the hardness of the

High Street. He got caught up in the mercenary madness as he bought an Instamatic in Boots. As he was buffeted by the hordes, he wondered would there be peace in the West Bank, in Bethlehem.

His last day in the office was interminable. The afternoon dragged; a dreary mist fell across the window. Passing time over a teacup with Fiona. She was asking about Mark; there was something there. Later packing his travelling bag with tee shirts and jeans. The night before flying out he was going to spend at Aunt Una's in London. The mist had multiplied when he finally caught the train at five.

Snatches of Christmas conversations on the Underground. Glossy ads glorifying plastic people. He read the meaningless messages to avoid the insolent eyes of a scut of skinheads. The rain had eased when he got out at Queen's Park. The night was quiet, the streets bleak. Only one old man shuffled past him as he walked to his Aunt's. He held a carrier bag in one hand. He was looking in doorways, searching for a home. So, this was 'The Streets Of London.' The last loneliness. The longest.

Aunt Una had kept dinner for him, but he could only pick at it. He felt, suddenly, tired and ventured to bed at ten. Angie was already in slumberland after hugging him goodbye. Timmie was in the Harp with his men and woke Liam up to say goodbye on his return. Afterwards, Liam lay awake listening to the night trains. The endless journeying.

Liam travelled in a dream during the night. A sadness shrouding his subconscious. He witnessed himself in stone silence staring for the last time through the front window at home. Rainclouds ebbing away the restless evening. The hills huddled on the horizon, defining darkness. The rain comes pelting down.

He looks at the clock on the mantlepiece, the one made in China. The time is twenty past nine. There is no knowing whether its morning or night. But he's leaving. His mother's face is drenched with tears. He reaches out but can't find her hand. He boards the morning bus. Passing through the soft shadow of the hills and into the nowhere of neon.

Another morning. Sounds seeping into his room. A child's voice; inarticulate tears. A train catching the echo of a tremor at the bedroom window. He draws the curtains across the day. Rain fading light finding the time on his watch.

He left in good time for Heathrow. He had to be there by midday although the flight wasn't until four. Israeli security had him open his carefully packed bag. They didn't quite understand his pronunciation of Kibbutz HaOgen as he explained the reason for his trip. His Hebrew was hairy! He ended up discussing the merits of his Nike Elite racers with one of them who did a bit of running. After moping around the concourse, the flight was finally called. He found a seat on the last coach across the tarmac.

He glanced once more at the grey sky and couldn't wait to leave London. Within ten minutes they were in the air. El Al: to the skies.

PART TWO

MY COUNTRY

I haven't sung thy praise
Nor glorified thy name
Nor rendered in tales of valour
And in war
Only a tree I plant
On Jordan's bank,
Only a path my feet have tracked
Across the fields.
Modest are the gifts I give you.
I know this, mother.
Modest I know the offerings of your daughter
Only an outburst of song
On a day when the light flares up,
Only a silent tear
For your poverty.

Rachel Bluwstein

Tel Aviv: Hill of the Springtime, littered with lights. The exited shouts of the passengers, craning their necks to catch a glimpse of the promised land. Outside of the city the land itself was clothed in darkness. Liam looked at his watch: eight in the evening. A difference in time touched his memory. It crossed his mind that when he used to go to Midnight Mass in his innocent days, it was a different time in Bethlehem. Deep and dark, lit only by his image of Israel.

The passengers were clapping. The pilot? He clapped with the old, assumed, Jewish lady in the next seat. She was going home, beaming. They had engaged in conversation at the start of the flight when he buckled her seat belt. She asked him did he know that the Israeli's bought the land of Palestine from the Arabs in 1948.He didn't know what to say; she believed it. Bought it alright, Liam thought, with blood. He mentioned the Balfour declaration, but she dismissed it with an intolerant hand.

After the meal was served; Kosher according to the woman, she taught him a few Hebrew expressions. 'Shalom for hello, for goodbye and for peace.'

She insisted he take a sweet from a paper bag. He obliged; she wasn't one to argue with!

'Todah-rabah'

'Thank you very much.'

She enunciated slowly for his benefit.

That's me fluent so, Liam smiled to himself.

They flew through Customs and Liam took his first breath of Israeli air. Soft and warm like late Summer. The taxi driver sensed his indecision. His ears were assaulted by sundry sounds. He thought he'd add a strange word to the pantomime himself.

'HaOgen. Near Netanya,' the city nearest the kibbutz. He asked how much, and the price of 1000 Israeli pounds threw him. He expected him to say shekels. He waited in the taxi checking his wallet; he had American dollars as well as Israeli currency. The taxi man came back to explain that he was waiting to see if anyone else was going to Netanya. If they were, Liam would get a discount for waiting.

The night air changed, chilled as they were on their way. No discount then, Liam thought. The taxi man asked for a cigarette. Liam told him no as he was an athlete. Liam made a running motion with his arms, but the man thought he was a racing driver.

The taxi stopped along the way for cigarettes and the driver bought Liam a packet of chewing gum as a compensation. Liam could make out the dark Mediterranean, on the route to Haifa. On the other side of the road there were flashing lights. A roadblock with traffic trailing back a distance.

'Special police,' the driver informed him. As they were driving through a town, Netanya, Liam thought, he saw young boys in military fatigues. They looked like boy scouts but were in fact the army of Israel.

The driver assured Liam that they wouldn't all be in bed; he had worked on a kibbutz himself. They came to a sign, but Liam couldn't make out the writing. The driver turned around recklessly in the middle of the road. HaOgen Road leading to a gate with a hut inside. A guard came out, a rifle slung over his shoulder. There ensued a conversation in Hebrew and they were ushered through the gate.

When Liam got out there was a smell of oranges mixed with silage in the air. The driver wouldn't leave before Liam was settled in. He knocked on the door of a small house, the volunteer leaders. A youngish woman came to the door and Liam listened to another barrage of Hebrew.

'I'm Offra, Shalom,' she smiled in the door light.

'You're Mark's friend.'

'Another runner,' she told the driver who was nodding.

'Yes. I'm Liam, what's another runner?' he agreed.

'Welcome to our kibbutz, Liam,' she held out her hand.

Liam tried his 'tow da' and her smile turned audible.

Laughing at my pronunciation, Liam thought. She excused herself to get some keys and Liam paid for the taxi.

When the driver had gone Offra emerged and led the way up a yard to a low roofed building. Inside there was a jumble of jeans and jumper on shelves. Above a cluttered desk was a picture of a wolf and a lamb captured in a furrowed field.

Waiting for the time: 'when the wolf also shall dwell with the lamb and they shall beat their swords into ploughshares.'

Offra picked out a couple of sheets and pillowcases from a pile in a laundry basket. She gave Liam a quilt to carry and she locked the door behind them. In the starlit darkness Liam could see a pen packed with cows. The smell of silo soured the air. Offra led the way up a flight of wooden steps to what looked like twin huts. A paraffin heater inside the door; socks drying on a boiler by a second door. Offra knocked on the first door calling 'Jan'.

'He's Swedish, ' she said to the questioning look on his face.

He had a momentary gender quandary. A sleep filled voice answered in English. Offra explained that this was Liam his new roommate.

'That's good,' came from within.

The door opened and a Scandinavian stereotype stood there. Big bodied, blonde haired and blue eyed.

Jan had spent the last five years as a volunteer in various kibbutzim. As Offra was making up the spare bed Liam asked did he know Mark. He told Liam that there was a party up in Switzerland and Mark was probably there, necking beers if not birds. Liam asked him what he worked at in Sweden and he was told that he was a psychiatric nurse. Liam thought, unkindly, that explains the re-location of Switzerland to the Middle East.

When Offra had finished with the bed she told Liam to call at the volunteer office in the morning. Pushing his bag under the bed Liam started to undress. Jan had already got under the covers as he had to be at the dairy at six. Just as they had said goodnight there was a commotion outside and poor Jan had to get up again. A knock and Mark stood there in his denims and donkey jacket, much too big for his slim frame. Liam sat up and Mark came over with his hand out.

'Watcha, mate.'

'Welcome to paradise!'

'Sorry for the intrusion.'

'I can't believe you're here.'

'It's beyond me as well,' Liam extended his hand.

'Where did you land that get-up,' Liam was pointing at his gear.

'The volunteer office issue, better than some of my own clobber.'

Liam asked where Mark's quarters were, hoping he wouldn't say anything silly like Zurich.

'About 800m up the kibbutz, it's called Switzerland, after the head volunteer there.

Liam nodded, intelligently at this explanation. Jan was sitting up in bed and said, 'we have a different name for ours.'

'What not Sweden mate? Bloody hell the Scandies are taking over,' Mark pretended to be peeved.

'No mister mate, I call it Shalom Shack, because that's what it is, a shack but maybe not shalom?'

'Not tonight anyway,' Jan was anxious to get back to sleep.

Jan turned off the light when Mark left, and Liam slipped into his hardboard bed. He could hear the animals lowing in the night and lay awake, jet lagged and jaded. He was awakened by a voice herding the cows in Hebrew. He drew back the curtain to a summer blue sky. A strange feeling as if the seasons had turned. He noticed that the windows were reinforced by mesh wire on the inside. As he was dressing Mark arrived to take him to Offra's office. There he was issued with the kibbutz uniform: Jeans, tee shirt and large jacket. Offra said 'the early mornings were cooled.'

She had trouble getting him a pair of boots that fitted, and he had to wear two pairs of socks.

After a brief breakfast of cheese, yogurt and coffee Mark had to go to work on avocados. Offra had given Liam the day off to settle in. As the following day was Shabbat his first working day was Sunday. Sunday? He would start in Pardes, picking oranges. Mark said he'd call for him at five for a run. The volunteers were like the United Nations: Swedish, Dutch, German, Swiss, Brits, Americans, North and South.

Outside, Liam was conscious of the sun and the season had suddenly summered. The warm, blue sky hung hazy over the citrus trees. He wondered, were the dusty, distant hills the summit of Samaria? He walked back to his room, in Shalom Shack, to unpack. The sun drew him out again and he spent the afternoon wandering around the perimeter. Doll designed houses bordered by a citrus forest. The children's house was the brightest.

Glints of green as the breeze stirred the trees. Sweet smell blowing along the orange groves. Beyond what he got used to calling 'Pardes,' the flat fields stretched to join another kibbutz. No fence or fear separated them. A cluster of wildflowers gathered in the green plain beyond. The Plain of Sharon where kibbutz Mishmar Ha Sharon sheltered.

'I am the lily of Sharon and the rose of the valley.'

The lyrical loveliness of the Song of Solomon before his eyes.

The sound of singing came from a multi-coloured building. The Children of the Dream? The book Sarah waved goodbye to him in Summerhill. Alongside lay the children's quarters where they slept, separate from their parents. The afternoon wore on; the sun softened, and a cool cloud carried a chill to his bare arms.

Liam started back making the dining hall his guide. Mark called on cue, they'd be doing an interval session at a track in Emek Hefer. A bus took them around the nearby kibbutzim, gathering up the athletes. A strong, agricultural smell hung over the track. While Mark cut out ten 400's Liam just jogged to get his jet-lagged legs back. His breath laboured lightly; his legs were lethargic. The night fell suddenly, and they returned to the bus.

On the way back, the young Israeli's were hurling Hebrew at each other. Darkness was complete over the kibbutz when they stepped off the bus. After a searing shower Liam headed for the dining hall. Out of season salad, chicken and pasta and copious cups of coffee. The volunteers ate in segregation from the kibbutz members. Some of the volunteers were learning Hebrew and Liam recognised a few phrases as they practiced at the meal.

Liam had a week to acclimatise before the race. Mark called for a morning run on Saturday, mimicking the marathon starting time. Behind him was a tall figure which Mark introduced as Gunther, his kibbutz training partner. Liam felt the jetlag lifting as they raced around the orange groves for a sharp 10k. Mark started his carbo loading at the Shabbat meal that night; pasta for five days. One more long run and they would be tapering for the race.

Liam felt strange to be working on a Sunday. There were two Swedish girls picking from a tree next to him. Their skimpy hot pants riding up the ridge of their buttocks as they reached for the oranges. Tight tops with 'Shalom' written across their prominence.

A cold rain was falling when Mark called for their last long run, this time around the avocado plot. An electrical storm followed with flashes of lightening and bursts of thunder.

Liam's heart sunk when he awoke with a sore throat and headache. Of all the times? He got through the day and went straight to bed on his return. He was dozing when Mark called for a short run.

'Sorry, I'm going down with some bug. Off you go!' He raised himself off the bed.

'Rotten luck chap; better tomorrow, hopefully.'

'Too close for comfort, bad timing,' Mark headed off with Gunther loping along behind him.

Liam toughed out the work in Pardes for the next two days. Mark got a packet of headache tablet from the kibbutz nurse for him.

'Missing a couple of days now is nothing; might be in your favour, we're only ticking over ourselves,' Mark reassured him.

Then it was Thursday: Marathon day.

5:45 Marathon morning; dining hall closed so banana and water for breakfast. Stars in the sky as Liam walked down to the kibbutz gate. There was a strong German team on the coach.

Daylight stretched slowly over the Plain of Sharon as they headed north.

The athletes were silent. They listened to the coach radio. The Voice of Peace.

'No more war, no more bloodshed.'

'Peace is the word.'

'And this is the Voice of Peace, 24 hours a day.'

They pass through the Hellenistic city of Beit Shean close to the 1967 border with Jordan. Directly south lie the conquered hills of Judea and Samaria. By 8:30 they glimpse the blinding blue waters of Galilee. At Ein Gev they're directed to change in a caravan.

There was a panic over the allocation of the numbers. Liam finally got his, number 282 from a Danish runner, mistaken identity? On the road outside there was a kaleidoscope of colour as they jogged to the start. This was a short warm-up, only time for a couple of strides. Liam lined up at the back of the 350 starters; Mark was in the elite group at the front. Liam shook hands with Mark and Gunther before the whistle start. The runners check their digitals: 9:30 on a sunny blue morning. False start: the elites were anxious.

Liam started at a casual pace. His legs felt tight, his throat dry. No adrenalin flowing; the waters of Galilee are still. He settled in the second group with two Israelis, a Swede and a Dane. Runners, united in the longest and loneliest race of all.

Repartee whilst running! Liam said very little in the exchanges. His legs began to loosen, and he relaxed into six-minute mile pace. The cool breeze around the lake freshened and cleared his head.

At 5k they came to the first drinks station. Grabbing a cup of water, it got up his nose as he tried to run and drink. He was flowing along now feeling better with every mile. The course led down to the kibbutzim in Lower Galilee. Children lined both sides of the narrow road and shout 'Yalla' and 'Mazel Tov'. Liam hoped they were meant to urge them on.

At 20k they saw the leaders coming back on the road south of the lake. German first, Italian second and Mark hanging on to them in third. The top Israeli, Yair Karni, who was born in HaOgen, was tenth. Liam gave him a shout; he knew him to see around the kibbutz.

At 25k the pace picked up; the intermediate field came back to them. Liam pushed on with only the Swede and one of the Israeli's going with him. He thought they might be on for a 2.45; not bad for a first marathon. At 30k he got a pulse down his left calf. Cramp? The battle with the gods of time and pain began. His right leg seized up from the hamstring to the calf. He had to stop, walking on the shore of the holy lake. The high sun was scorching the sweat on his face. He tried to rub the lump from his leg and began to jog.

After a time without movement or measure, runners seemed to fly past him. Yet they were barely moving and he responded but his legs would not answer. He took a cup at a drink's station; the cool water refreshed his mind. Passing through Tiberius he tried to hold his head up. Armed Israeli soldiers answered his indicating arm at a turn-off.

'Ken, yes, yalla, let's go!

The long road to Ginosar lay ahead. He was isolated now; a gap behind and a bigger one in front. He was looking for the sign for 40k written on the hot road. In the distance he saw people blurred by the sun. The road into the kibbutz was sheltered by a parade of banana trees on both sides. He saw the finishing line and effected a slow sprint. He limped like a wounded warrior over the line and was wrapped in a blanket. Sipping a cool orange drink, he was laid on a stretcher and given electrical pulses to relax the rock-like muscles.

Gasping at the blessed blue sky over Galilee he closed his eyes. Totting up the hundreds of miles for this moment. The lunchtime runs, the twenty miles on Sunday's. The dark and bitter winter nights. The ice, the snow, the relentless rain. The miles could never measure up to this moment of completion. Calvary conquered!

Liam was euphoric to finish inside three hours in the circumstances. Gunther had dipped inside 2.30 and Mark posted a 2.20 to finish third. Not bad for a training run as he put it. The presentation was held in an airy hall that looked like a basketball court. The walking wounded dragged themselves to a table near the food bar. A line of women lined up behind the bar to serve falafels and coffee.

When the winner was called, he got up from the next table; Werner Dorrenbecher, Mark recognised him, having kept pace with him for twenty miles. When he returned, they all stood up to shake his hand before Mark made his way to the podium for his bronze. The rest of the field got a medal just for finishing!

Afterwards there was a gymnastic display and when it was over two young girls approached. They were asking the winner for his autograph. As they turned to go Mark said, ' shalom there, what about us?' They looked at each other and one of them came back.

'You came third so sign please,' she held out her autograph book.

'And your country too'.

'England,' he said as he signed a little sheepishly.

'And you,' to Gunther.

'Tenth and Germany is my country,' he said seriously.

Finally, she turned her very pale blue eyes to Liam.

'I came nowhere, Ireland actually,'

'Mazel Tov. sign please,' she exclaimed.

'Pardon,' Mark was stumped.

'Congratulations.'

'Good luck,' she turned to her waiting friend.

'My Mama comes from Ireland,' she said over her shoulder.

'Oh, where?' Liam detained her.

'Cork,' and she was gone.

When the girls got back to the food bar they started to point in their direction. They were gathering their gear when the autograph hunter returned with a slim figured woman. Her fair hair like the girl bobbing in a ponytail behind her. Liam was reaching down painfully to retrieve his bag when he heard Mark speak.

'Well, shalom there again.'

The young girl was saying 'this is Leem and he's from Ireland, like you.'

'And this is Mark,' she read from her book.

'From England.'

'Ireland and England, together?'

When Liam raised his eyes, his heart skipped in his chest.

'It's Liam, isn't it?' the woman was looking straight into his eyes.

He could see the gold flecks flare in the emerald green. He knew straight away who stood before him, like an apparition.

'Sarah, I can't believe it!'

'Of all the places to meet again,' he found himself waffling.

He could see that Mark was looking from one to the other, enquiringly.

'Sorry Mark, this is Sarah. We used to know each other at home.'

Sarah shook Mark's hand and held out her hand again. Liam took her tiny hand in his, strangely formal.

'What a surprise,' she smiled into his eyes.

'Please Sarah, sit here, our friend has left.'

Gunther had moved over to speak to the German team. When she sat down Mark excused himself to check the coach for the return journey.

'I shall leave you two to catch up.'

And they were alone again, as unsure as the first time all those years ago.

'Inbar, you can sit here until Mark, is it, gets back.' Sarah indicated the empty chair.

When Inbar sat down she was smiling from one to the other.

'Inbar'? Is this young lady yours?' he could see the likeness.

'Yes, my daughter, my one and only.'

'Trust me one of her is enough,' and she tousled Inbar's fringe.

'I didn't know you were a runner.'

'Thought soccer was your sport,' Sarah turned in her seat.

'You're right, it was in Cork when I played for UCC,' he faced her.

'I only took up jogging when I emigrated; I'm in the UK now. England actually, where I met Mark and joined his athletic club.'

'I realised it was more my sports metier. Suits an outsider, remember?' he smiled.

'Yes, L'etranger,' she pronounced impeccably, again, smiling at the memory.

'We both seemed so serious then,' she added.

'Adolescent angst,' he laughed.

'Anyway, I guess we've outgrown all that. Different people now?' she posed.

'I suppose, though you're still the same Sarah to me,' he looked shyly at her.

'And you to me Liam despite the years,' she held his gaze.

'Still angsty though,' they burst out laughing.

Inbar was squirming in her seat trying to figure out what was so funny. She didn't often see her mother in this mood. She touched her daughter's arm and pointed to the food bar which looked like closing.

'Inbar, would you fetch a couple of coffees and an orange juice for yourself? '

'Please, before they shut the bar, there's a good girl.'

'Were you here just for the marathon?' Sarah queried.

'Yes, Mark got me out here as he's training in kibbutz HaOgen for the winter.'

'So, I'm staying for a month and also working in HaOgen if I've pronounced it properly.'

'Near enough and near me. We're near neighbours, me and Inbar live in kibbutz Mishmar Ha Sharon,' she smiled.

Mark returned with news of the coach's departure. Liam hesitated as Inbar came back with the coffees. Sarah said they could give Liam a lift back as she took the drinks from Inbar.

'Is that alright, Mark,' Liam was in two minds.

'No problem, mate, I'll let the driver know.'

'Like I said you have some catching up to do, cheers,' Mark shook Sarah's hand again and waved to Inbar.

'Never a truer word, he doesn't know the half of it,' Sarah smiled a little wanly.

Liam was thinking, neither do I.

After the coffees they headed off in the darkness. Inbar was asleep in the back seat by the time they reached HaOgen Road. Liam was telling Sarah he hoped to return to Galilee and see it more slowly than six-minute mileing.

'I'm off for the weekend and if you like I could drive to Tiberius,' Sarah volunteered.

'That's terrific, we're also off until Monday, to recover,' he was delighted.

'How far are you from Netanya,' he enquired.

'About 5k, why?'

'How about me buying you lunch tomorrow as a down payment for the trip?'

'Fine,' she agreed instantly.

'Pick you up about midday?'

'Perfect, but what about your young lady?'

'Basketball in Beit Shean, isn't it Inbar?' she addressed the sleepy form.

A muffled 'yes Mama' came from Inbar.

Sarah dropped him by the security gate and arranged to pick him up again at midday. That sweet smile again he thought as she said goodbye. A sleepy 'Shalom' came out of the darkness in the back seat. When he got out of the car the stiffness seized him. He literally had to drag his heavy legs up the steps to Shalom Shack. He let the hot water from the shower massage his calves, wishing he could have a soak in Epsom salts, as usual.

Jan had gone to Netanya in a Sherut with his pal from the dairy. Staying overnight for Shabbat and dining out on steak and Arak beer. Not quite kosher?

Afterwards he lay down for a doze, running the race through his mind. Hitting the wall at eighteen miles meant he hadn't done enough long runs. Along with his illness and the 800m over distance they had run he couldn't be too disappointed with his run. It was Mark who found out that the course was changed due to flooding after the storm. Times had to be adjusted; the Einstein amongst them more generous to themselves. The five-minute milers knocking two and a half minutes off. This would have given Mark a sub 2.15 and Liam a modest three minutes better. We wondered what the winner must be thinking with a personal best on.

'Never again,' he'd said to Mark, but runners often say that until they forget the pain.

He thought of the surreal appearance of Sarah. Was that a premonition of more pain? She would have made new friends;

maybe married a stranger. He decided not to ask but wait for her to tell.

In the morning he tried a walk cum jog around the orange groves. The lactic eased from his muscles after a half hour. He even ran a few strides at the finish, his legs like lead as he lifted his knees.

The sun was closeted by clouds all morning but escaped as Sarah pulled up by the dining hall. She watched him shuffling, painfully, down the steps of Shalom Shack.

'How do you put yourselves through all that pain?' her lovely eyes were concerned.

'We must be the original masochists,' he grinned, pulling one leg after the other into the car.

Sarah was wearing blue jeans and a white top, her colours now. This 'daughter of Israel'. There was a blue motif of the Israeli flag pronouncing her breasts. She was driving a pale blue car whose make Liam didn't recognise. When he remarked on its unusual design, she told him it was the first Israeli car made in Haifa. The iconic Sabra Sussita called after an ancient city east of the Sea of Galilee, now an archaeological site.

Her slim buttocks jigged in her jeans as he followed her down the escalator to Netanya beach.

They had lunch in Cafe Café. Liam was mulling over the name 'so good they named it twice,' like New York by two! Sarah ordered the staple diet of young Israel, falafel and coffee.

'Only for Inbar looking for the marathon winner's autograph we probably would have never met again,' Sarah said as they settled down.

'I know, unreal or surreal even; another miracle in Galilee,' he smiled.

'Oh right,' she was unsure.

'But miracle or not it's lovely to see you again, Liam,' she held out her hand.

'Me too,' he squeezed her tiny palm.

After lunch Sarah suggested a walk along Netanya beach. Her hand brushed his as they walked closely amongst the Shabbat crowd. On the way back to HaOgen she invited him to the evening meal in Mishmar. He gave her a quick peck on the cheek as they parted.

'Back at seven,' she touched his cheek.

When she dropped him off the runners were gathering at the dining hall for the evening run. Changing quickly, he caught up with the stragglers. He could make out Mark ahead; he could pick out that bouncing style in a pack. He felt heavy after the lunch and just jogged for twenty minutes.

The evening was closing in when she drove through the security gate. He recognised the Sabra gliding like a sleek horse, Sussita.

The sun reddening the orange groves; the fruit hanging like decorations on a Christmas tree. Inbar wanted to show 'Leem' around their kibbutz, her school, the basketball court. The three of them strolling into the sunlit silence of Shabbat. The two blonde heads as if in highlights, close together with Inbar linking them both. On the way back from the back fields Sarah pointed out a multi-coloured building. This is where she worked with the 'Children of the Dream'.

There were prayers said, in Hebrew, at the start of the evening meal. Sarah and Inbar bowed their heads beside him. Pasta again Liam thought as the main meal was served. They had a bottle of Mount Tabor Chardonnay and Sarah raised a toast.

'To Ireland, Israel, Palestine,' she surprised him.

In some ways a tragic trinity. She let Inbar have a sip of her wine and clinked Liam's glass.

'Cheers.'

'What's the toast they make in Ireland, Mama,' Inbar took an empty glass.

'Slainte,' Sarah smiled.

'You haven't lost the old vernacular,' Liam laughed.

The dining hall had emptied by the time they left. Sarah invited him back to their house for a coffee as the evening cold hit them.

'I've heard that one before; is that a euphemism,' he joked on the way.

'No, just Israeli instant,' she shot back.

Inbar was looking at them wondering what the joke was. Adults!

Liam put his gear into a small backpack before going to bed. Just in case they found a place for a run; a habit runners had. Afraid to miss a training session. He struggled to get off, sleep coming late, his legs restless. Wondering about Sarah; she now had a daughter.

He met Mark on the way back from his morning run and told him he was returning to Galilee with Sarah. She was turning the Sabra around when he left Shalom Shack with his backpack.

She still took his breath away as he glanced sideways at her face in profile. In a couple of hours, they were rolling into Tiberius.

Sarah suggested a cycle around the lake for perhaps a couple of hours. Then she said she knew a quaint restaurant to eat in the evening. She also had a friend, Yanina, at Ein Gev and arranged showers on their return. The man in the shop told them they could easily cycle to Capernaum, 10k away.

They were both a bit rusty; Sarah wobbled to begin with, and Liam had trouble engaging the gears. Liam was trying to remember what happened at Capernaum. The feeding of the five thousand? They arrived in Tabgha in a steady hour and stopped outside a church. Reading the sign Liam realised he had got his Catechism wrong. The Church of the Multiplication. The maths miracle of the loaves and fishes.

It was lunchtime when they got to Capernaum. Sarah spotted the remnants of a synagogue. Jesus would have attended there, as a Jew. So, did Judaism predate Christianity? Liam wondered seeing as Jesus was first a Jew. Sarah was looking sad as she left, the ruin lay like an admonishment to history. He put his arm round her shoulder for a moment without words. She said 'sorry, but I was thinking of my first synagogue at home in South Terrace.' Her mother told her that the numbers attending were falling gradually. Before too long it too would be as empty as the ruin in Capernaum.

They parked their bikes without locking them, like it used to be in Ireland when Liam was a boy. After visiting the

Monastery of the Beatitudes, they found a small cafe nearby. Over a quick snack of croissants and coffee Sarah asked him did he ever hear what Capernaum was called.

'Not a notion,' he answered.

'The city of Jesus,' she replied.

'I would have said Nazareth or Bethlehem instead,' he admitted.

Finishing their snack, they jumped on their bikes and headed back to Tiberius.

The glacial glint of the evening sun was starting to set over Galilee. A soft breeze was brushing the gold hinted waves. Out of the blue 'Innisfree' came to mind for Liam. He started quoting Yeats to Sarah.

'I will arise and go now, for always night and day

I hear lake water lapping with sweet sound by

the shore;

While I stand on the roadway, or on the

pavement grey,

I hear it in the deep heart's core.'

Her flushed face turned, smilingly, towards him as they cycled side by side. Her burnished fair hair flying away behind her the blonde had paled to pallid over the years.

'Sweet sound to go with your sweet smile,' he held out his hand.

They cycled one handed until an irate Israeli driver tooted them to single file.

When they got back to Tiberius they drove to Ein Gev where the marathon had started. Liam walked down to the edge of the lake while Sarah was showering. He imagined Jesus, walking along that same shore. He was, almost, returning to his boyhood when he could believe.

He was pitched out of his reverie when Sarah put a hand on his shoulder.

'A shekel for your thoughts,' she smiled.

'Hardly worth them,' he covered her hand.

'Offer withdrawn then,' she took her hand away. 'Shall we take a little walk along the shore before you shower?' she asked.

'Yes, let's!' he touched her arm.

The sun was like a golden ball on the far side of the lake. The breeze was stilled on the water as if it were in repose. He wanted to hold her hand as they walked to the border of the kibbutz. A peaceful silence came over them. Her hand was swinging, and he caught it and covered it with his. She smiled and gave a little squeeze, her shoulder brushed against his. As they turned at the far end of the shore they came together. Her lips gleamed as he reached down and touched them gently. She came into his arms and they held each other as if they would never let go. Alone on the shore of the holy lake they were together again.

The sinking sun was spreading embers along the gentle water. By the time they had walked back dusk was only delayed by a ribbon of red around the lake. Sarah went to Yanina's house to change and came back with two coffees while Liam showered. When he emerged, he had changed into the gear he had brought, red and black, his club colours. Sarah had brought a blue and white dress in a holdall. The Star of David unfurled across the bodice. They sat outside on a bench and drank the lukewarm coffees in the fading warmth of the declining sun. They drove into the centre of Tiberius and parked opposite the quaint restaurant called Little Tiberius.

Liam let her order the wine, speaking in Hebrew to the waitress. She chose a bottle of Golan Heights Emerald Riesling.

'It's like St. Patrick's Day with the green beer, cheers,' he clinked her glass.

'Shabbat Shalom,' her oval face was animated. 'I still can't believe how we met again after all these years,' she held out her hand.

He was a bit taken aback and held it for a moment.

'Isn't life strange, like the turn of a page; lovely to see you again Sarah,' he eased her hand back.

'And Inbar; I never imagined you would have a daughter.'

'Inbar? What does it mean in Hebrew,' he wanted to know more.

'Well, I used to think it meant jewel,' she laughed. 'But it actually means amber,' she pulled a face.

'However, it means jewel in Arabic; a rare gemstone with a warm honey shade,' she added.

'She's my little jewel anyway but rare,' she smiled fondly.

'You might say that she's an amber jewel in that case,' Liam raised his glass.

'You know, she looks just like you when I first saw you in Summerhill,'

'So, people tell me,' she poured another glass. Their fingers touched as she held his glass to pour. She took a breath almost like a sigh. Her lips parted before a hesitant whisper escaped.

'But she has your eyes,' her lashes came down like a curtain.

Liam sat back his glass half raised, then put it down banging the table. Was he hearing things? Mistaken the whispered words. His heart shunted in his chest. His breath caught in his throat.

'My daughter? Inbar?'

'Yes,' the small word confirmed.

Eyes descending under her lashes for a moment. Blinking she raised them again, the flecks like liquid gold.

'Our daughter,' she said this time clearly.

Liam reached across for her hand, tiny in his. 'I don't know what to say. Sorry is not enough. I had no idea.' he searched her face.

For what? For forgiveness?

'Me neither,' a lost look in her eyes.

'I didn't know how to tell you. It just came out when you mentioned Summerhill and compared us.'

'I'm not sure now whether I should have.'

'I don't want you to feel burdened. We have different lives now, worlds apart. Then again, you have a right to know. Inbar is our own flesh and blood. Nothing can change that reality.'

When she finished her eyes misted in the candlelight. He was feeling smaller and smaller as he listened silently.

After all these years in different times. A summer's night in Mayfield. Scattered seed gathering fruit in Galilee. Inbar harvested like 'the lily of the valley and the rose of Sharon'. Liam could feel a literal lump in his throat. They were both shaken, hands still entwined, shocked into silence.

When the chicken and pasta was served Liam filled their glasses with the Emerald Riesling.

'A toast to our daughter, to Inbar.'

It felt strange saying 'daughter'. Sarah raised her glass to his, looking relieved as if a burden were lifted.

When the waitress returned Sarah asked for the dessert menu in Hebrew. She could revert to English in a breath, the Cork inflection still apparent.

Liam was itching to ask a question. A worry at the back of his mind.

'Sarah,' he stopped.

'Yes, what is it?'

It was as if she knew what was coming.

'Does Inbar know?'

'No, not yet.'

'She's only twelve and coming up to the age when her hormones will be hurtling around her body.'

'Hurling hormones as we might say in Cork,' she lightened the moment.

'However, I fully intend to tell her when she's eighteen.'

'She will be away with the IDF by then.'

'The army?'

'Yes, IDF means the Israeli Defence Force which is compulsory.'

'At eighteen they all serve and swear an oath 'Masada shall never fall'.'

'Besides, she had a father, a surrogate you might say.'

'This was when she was quite young, a child.'

'So, as far as Inbar is concerned Haim was her father.'

Sarah was very measured as she was explaining.

'Haim?' Liam was put out by the news and wondered about the past tense.

After a desert of fruit salad, they drained the wine before ordering two coffees. Liam got up to go to the loo and settled the bill on the way back. They sat in silence for a while before Sarah spoke again.

'Liam, I know you have a lot to take in and I have much more to tell. Besides the bombshell...sorry wrong word,' she seemed to regret saying it. 'So, only if you want, we can find a bar and I can tell the rest.'

'No, I would like to know more about your life since... you know'?

'But you don't have to tell me everything if it's private.'

'No secrets, except the one I surprised you with.'

When they entered the Choko bar there was only a handful of people. Finding a quiet table at the back they sat together on a long couch Sarah ordered a couple of Gold Star beers while Liam wondered what was to come.

'So, Sarah, what's the rest of the story?' Liam turned to face her.

When Liam was on that train to Kerry after his exams Sarah was flying to Tel Aviv. Working in the kindergarten in Beit Shean, her first kibbutz. She was a month there when she noticed that she had missed her time. Her principle sent her to a doctor in Netanya when she started to feel unwell. When she was sent for a test it came back positive. She remembered saying to the doctor 'but I can't be.' He replied, 'Well you are, unless it's another immaculate conception.' He then gave her the options to consider before making another appointment. Shocked to the core she returned to the kibbutz, her mind racing. How would she tell her mother, her father, her principal? Would she be allowed to remain on the kibbutz? Would she be welcomed at home especially by her Orthodox father?

She went straight to the school when she arrived back, and the principal took her into her little office. When Sarah told her, she passed the phone across her desk to ring home. The principal left her in private and went into their kitchen to make coffee. Her mother went quiet when she got the news but then asked her to come home. But her father felt that she had brought shame on the family. She had strayed from her people and the tenets of her faith.

It was the principal Mrs Rosenstein, like a surrogate mother who took Sarah under her wing. She informed the kibbutz committee on Sarah's behalf. There was no question of her having to abandon the kibbutz way of life. A communal agreement was reached that if Sarah wished she could transfer to another kibbutz when the time was right. Just before the six-day war she moved to Mishmar Ha Sharon to work in the children's house.

On a sunny morning in May a baby girl was born. The image of exile overflowing from her pale blue eyes. Inbar.

Sarah paused and Liam put an arm around her shoulder. How he wished he had been there for her, for their daughter. He knew he could never make amends for his absence. She leaned her head on his shoulder and closed her eyes before continuing.

'Ironically, I had planned to come home after my stint on the kibbutz. Before coming out I had applied to UCC for a place. My mother had sent me the acceptance letter from the Arts faculty. I wanted to study Literature, maybe Joyce, Yeats. Perhaps Hesse and Camus like you were reading that day in the Glen. L'etranger. But I was the outsider now.'

Liam was slowly sipping his beer, listening intently. Consumed with guilt, with sorrow. Enveloped in a shroud of sadness. For Sarah. For himself? Sarah straightened up and he removed his arm from her shoulder.

'Instead, I applied to get a teaching qualification to teach Hebrew in an Ulpan.' This was for the people who were making Alia to Israel. Hebrew was the bond that bound Israeli society. So, when I got my qualification a part time vacancy came up in Ulpan Netanya. So, I'm a kibbutznik by day and a teacher in the evenings.'

'And the rest is history,' she smiled, sipped her beer.

After a short time in Mishmar she was offered a small house; no more sharing a room, sometimes with the volunteers.

Shortly afterwards she had a new pupil in the Ulpan. Haim, a young man arrived on his own from Eastern Europe. He told Sarah, rather proudly that he came from Vilnius. Proud because it was called the Jerusalem of Lithuania. Her Superior later revealed that Haim had lost his family in Ponar Forest during the pogroms. When he was barely five years old his parents were shot by the Nazis. They were marched through Vilnius and thrown into a pit with the other one hundred thousand. His uncle was part of the Burning Brigade who were kept chained in the pits during the night. They were compelled to cremate their kindred; burn the evidence.

He became the twelfth man who survived the escape. They used spoons and their bare hands to burrow their way out. It was the last night of Passover when they reached the forest. It was he who rescued Haim and brought him up as his own son. His uncle, whom Haim called 'Papa' also paid for his Alia to Israel. He had no English and only a smattering of Hebrew. When he spoke quickly it sounded like Yiddish to Sarah. She signed him up for a course of Hebrew in her Ulpan. She told him he sounded like a Sabra, a native, when he had finished

Because of his farming background he was assigned to the dairy and looking after the herd. They would meet in the dining hall for the communal evening meal. Sometimes they would have a coffee afterwards and he would practice the language; able to laugh at his errors. When the calves were born, they would take Inbar to see them. He would hoist her up over the pens to touch their inquisitive noses which would send Inbar into gales of giggles.

One Shabbat evening in Netanya, Sarah bumped into Haim near the beach. He was walking on his own as always looking at the menus outside the cafes. She recommended one to him and he asked if she would join him. He told her he was sharing a room with a volunteer. Not much company with two different languages.

A few weeks later he was very subdued in the classroom. When Sarah asked if he was alright, he told her he had to share with a new volunteer, another language. That's when Sarah decided to offer him the spare bedroom and, in a week, he moved in. And Inbar had her 'Abba,' until the Yom Kippur war.

Haim was called up along with all the able bodied of both genders. After some initial training he was posted to the Golan Heights which was annexed by Israel. The stray bullet that tore into him came from the direction of the retreating Syrian soldiers. Ethan, a young Seraphim from North Africa he had befriended fell with him. There were rumours that the soldiers mutilated the bodies of their enemies.

Sarah was trying to tell what was done to Haim's body.

'They severed...you know...and stuffed it into his mouth. He was just into his prime and his comrade only eighteen,'

Liam put his arm around her shoulder. She turned her face, and he swept her tears with his other hand.

'Sarah please, you don't have to tell me anymore,' he touched her cheek with his wet hand.

When she composed herself, she calmy told him the rest.

How she had to go up to Kiryat Shmona to identify the body. So impersonal... the body. How his Company brought him back to the kibbutz. The sealed coffin shrouded in the Israeli flag. The price paid for Masada; that it would not fall again. All work except the dairy and the kitchen stopped on the kibbutz for the funeral. Because Haim had no family with him an army rabbi chanted the Kaddish. Most kibbutzim have their own cemetery and he was buried in Kfar Haim. The similar names weren't lost on those present. A strange coincidence as if the grave were named for him.

Sarah found it difficult to tell Inbar that Haim, her 'Abba' wasn't coming home. When Sarah said her 'Abba' she made the inverted comma sigh with her fingers. Inbar had got to calling Haim 'Papa', because all her school pals had fathers. Neither Sarah nor Haim had the heart to correct her.

'That's the end of my story,' she smiled with what seemed relief.

'Sometimes I think I'll wake up and find it all a dream. Or a nightmare more likely,' she forced a wan smile.

'I'm so sorry, you've been through the wars in more ways than one,' Liam took his arm from her shoulder.

'Excuse me, I must find the ladies,' she reached for her handbag.

'Shall I get a brandy on the way back?'

'I think we need it, you anyway.'

'So yes, please.'

Glancing at his watch he was surprised at how late it was. He finished his beer as she returned.

'It's getting on,' he took a taste.

'Ok, let's make a start after this,' she shuddered as she sipped.

She touched his arm lightly and touched his glass.

'To happier times,' she smiled.

The tear troubled smudges had been wiped from her face in the ladies.

'To be with you is happy enough for me,' his throat burned.

'I'm sorry but you are the only one I could tell about Haim.' It spilled out like a dam bursting.' I couldn't even tell my mother. As for my father ...,' she trailed off. 'Thanks again for listening to me and my travails.'

'It couldn't have been easy with Inbar calling Haim 'Papa,'' she touched his cheek.

He held her hand there without a word.

Liam didn't want the night to end despite everything he learned. He was trying to find the words before they got to the car.

'Sarah, could we find a couple of rooms and stay the night in Tiberius.'

'It would be safer than driving with vino in the veins.'

'And we' re both wiped out with the day that's in it,' he looked expectantly at her.

'If you wish as Inbar is sleeping over at her best friend's.'

'She's the one you saw with her after the marathon, twelve going on twenty!'

'They're like two Sabra's in a pot; prickly on the outside but sweet on the inside,' she laughed at the image.

'Besides, aren't we all off tomorrow?' she looked relieved.

'Let's try the Lake House Kinneret Hotel." She was reaching for the car keys in her handbag.

The reception was cool and quiet, either air conditioning or a night breeze from Galilee. The only vacancy was a twin-bedded room. Sarah looked at him enquiringly.

'If it's good by you,' he hesitated.

'Fine so,' Sarah signed them in.

'Was it the Israeli equivalent of Mr and Mrs Smith,' he joked in the lift.

'Well, you're Mr Cohen for the night,' she said back.

The initial shyness and tension dissipated before they reached the room. The beds were joined together and Liam went to separate them.

'I didn't want you to think you could take advantage of me,' he smiled.

'As if?' she said over her shoulder on the way to the bathroom.

Liam sat on the far side of his bed and wondered should he sleep in his gear. When Sarah came out of the bathroom, she was wearing a long baggy sweater with her dress folded over her arm. She gave a little twirl before sitting on the edge of her bed.

'Chic or what? Your turn.'

'What,' he ruffled her wet hair as he passed.

'Thanks,' she called after him.

When he returned, she was in bed with the duvet up to her chin. He turned off the main light and slipped into bed with his gear still on. The diffused glow of the bedside lamps spread shadows around the ceiling. They reached up together and turned the lights off.

'Thanks for a lovely day.'

'I hope I didn't spoil it with my troubles,' her voice emerged from the darkness.

'Not at all. I've always wondered what happened to you.'

'I'm only sorry I couldn't have been there for you and for Inbar. I feel so guilty now...' he stopped. 'If we hadn't ...you know ...'

She reached across her hand and found his cheek.

'I don't regret that night in Mayfield.'

'We must have been lonely for each other.'

'I loved you.'

He reached up and took her hand, holding it between the twin beds.

'I'm still lonely for you, still love you, Sarah.'

He could feel tears tug at his eyelids. Only their hands were bridging the silence, articulating their feelings in the darkness.

'Thank you,' she released her hand.

'Well, goodnight then,' she said softly.

'Sleep well,' he turned over.

When he awoke, Sarah's head was resting on his shoulder her hand flung across his chest. Her body was stretched diagonally on the bed. He covered her shoulders gently with his duvet. She awoke with a start and blinked her eyes into his withdrawing her hand.

'Chara!'

'Zoobie!' she swore.

'Pardon?'

'Were you cursing?'

'Yes, sorry,' she looked sheepish.

'Not too strong I trust for a lady?'

'No, the equivalent of 'feck and 'shite' at home.'

'That's alright so, like holy Hebrew.' he sat up.

'Any excuse!'

'I thought I was in grave moral danger there.'

'Too late for that methinks.'

It's just that I'm so used to having the bed to myself,' she shuffled over the gap.

After a quick shower they were on their way to Nazareth. Sarah insisted on paying citing the hogging of the beds.

'And hugging me as a bonus,' he said as they reached the car.

'Modesty becomes you,' she retorted with a smile.

Galilee was letting light spread over its waves. The sun perched on the summit of a hill. Mount Tabor? Filtering down to soften the contours of the valley. Jezreel? Liam wished that his geography was better; realising how little he knew of Israel, of Judaism.

As they drove the light spread slowly and drew the clouds from the sky. Liam took one last look at the wending waves of Galilee. It had made some atavistic impression on him that belonged to his boyhood. The holy lake blessed in the boyhood of Jesus. Sarah had noticed; it was a special place to him now.

It was getting on for ten when they arrived in Nazareth. Liam could see a church with a cupola in the distance. As they drove nearer, he could make out the inverted lily and lantern: The Church of the Annunciation. Sarah waited outside and parked the car while he entered. In the quietness, only a few Arab women were kneeling. In the vast silence he sat on a seat near the altar. No prayer would come so he lit an electric candle, thinking of Haim.

When he emerged, Sarah was standing back trying to capture the whole church with his Instamatic.

'Duty done,' he explained the candle lighting ritual to her.

'I understand the symbolism,' she said on the way to the car.

'Of course.'

'I remember; you were lighting the Hannukah candles the evening we met. Instead of coming to the pictures in the Lee with me,' he reproached gently.

'Spiritual priorities,' she dug her small fist, playfully, into his arm.

'Fair enough, I suppose we had our own hard day's night after meeting again in the Shambles,' he put an arm lightly around her shoulder.

'I'd say, very hard,' she circled his waist until they reached the car.

They had a light breakfast in the Moka cafe, just croissants and coffee. He asked her how it was she knew so much about his religion and he so little about hers. She told him that all her friends in Cork would be going to church while she was going to the synagogue with adults, only. When the school was preparing the children for First Communion she was excused. She so wanted to wear the white dress her best friend would wear. She even asked her mother why she couldn't be like her friends even for a day. Her mother gently explained that she was born into Judaism like generations of her family. But her mother gave her money to give to her best friend and they had a photograph taken. The white dress with the cross motif contrasting with the blue with the Star of David, their shoulders close together.

It was early afternoon when they passed through Caesarea and on to Hadera. Soon they turned into HaOgen Road and pulled up outside the security hut. Sarah showed her ID to the guard; Liam just nodded. Learning from Mark not to say anything to security. They were serious citizens, ex-military.

When Sarah dropped him off by the dining hall Gene was just knocking off after the early shift on Big Dishes. Liam whispered they call him 'Hygiene' and spelled it out.

'Unfortunate name for one doing kitchen work,' she stifled a giggle.

Liam resisted and called out 'Hello, Gene.'

'Hi Liam,' he was staring at Sarah as he spoke.

Liam introduced them and they shook hands through the driver's window.

When Gene loped off Liam told her that Mark used to say American's don't do irony. They merely think it's an element!

They both hesitated; was this goodbye again? A silence lingered in the air.

'Well, Shalom again,' Sarah held out her hand.

'Thanks for taking me back to Galilee, and the rest,' he took her hand.

'You're welcome, my pleasure with a fair bit of pain thrown in,' she left her hand in his.

' Sarah, I... I don't want to say goodbye here. Would you be able to have dinner with me before I fly back on Thursday?'

'Fine, when do you have in mind?' She slipped her hand free.

'I'm working Sunday and Monday and we're due to go to Jerusalem and Bethlehem for Christmas Eve.'

'So, Tuesday in Netanya?'

'Also, I'd like to be able to say 'goodbye' to Inbar.'

'I think she has a gymnastic lesson in Mishmar on Tuesdays.'

'So, after dinner we could detour back home before dropping you off to HaOgen.'

'Perfect,' he captured her hand in a formal goodbye.

When he hauled himself up to Shalom Shack, he felt dog tired. He lay down on the hard bed, his mind reeling. Alone, he tried to internalise all the information Sarah had disseminated. Process the pain that Sarah had endured, because of him? Guilt enveloping him like a vice. Drifting off; waking as if it was all a dream.

Daylight was waning when he pulled on his tracksuit. He was just in time for the evening run and fell in with Gunther. The pace was set like a metronome by Mark. Liam's head cleared as his legs eased out over the 10k loop. The sun was skimming over the orange grove to set as they finished in darkness.

The Shabbat meal was the best one of the week. Candles were lit and bottles of wine were breathing on the tables.

Liam sat with Mark with a couple of Swedish girls between them. Mark had spent the day with them on avocados.

'You're a dark horse mate,' Mark whispered across the girls.

120

'What, who?' Liam said innocently.

'I thought you came out to do a marathon, not to run into an old flame?' Mark wasn't letting up.

'Well, I was just as surprised...I ...' he trailed off.

'You finally got a nickname anyway.'

'Lothar,' Mark was grinning.

'What? They think I'm Gunther's brother?'

'Na, short for Lothario.'

'Me? Highly unlikely. Not with my record with women,' they were both laughing.

Mark said that's how the volunteers amused themselves, giving each other nicknames.

When they were on their own Liam told Mark about meeting Sarah in Cork. Not touching on different religions, cultures, worlds. Nor about Inbar or Haim, only the bare bones. When he had finished Mark was silent for a moment.

'Shame, you two look made for each other,' he got up to go.

The blonde and brunette Swedish girls, nicknamed Abba, were having another party in Switzerland. They linked Mark on either side like he was their prisoner. Liam declined, relieved to get back to the peace of Shalom Shack.

The next morning started grey and cold, the sun hidden by a wall of cloud. Liam went through the motions for the six hours work. Mark was king of the avocados again with the Swedish girls. Nobody seemed to know what Gunther did - not a hint - as they only saw him running.

It was hard to believe it was Christmas Eve. Not a sign of holly or 'holy' as someone said. But they'd be going to where it all started in a couple of hours.

It was the Pardes manager, Moshe, who counted the volunteers into the minibus. It was early evening when the ochre-coloured walls of Jerusalem came into view. They entered by Jaffa Gate, one of the six or seven in the Old City. The blocked up Golden Gate, the Gate of Mercy was believed to be the entrance to paradise. Temple Mount was teeming with people circled by armed Israeli soldiers. A hum was coming from the Wailing Wall. Paper prayers were being pushed into crevices. Men and women rocking back and forth, separately. A gold halo hung over the Dome of the Rock; the Al-Aqsa mosque sedate in the evening glow. Liam heard one of the Swiss volunteers ask, ' what are all those shoes outside for?'

'Jesus wept,' Mark couldn't believe his ears.

'Perhaps not Jesus,' Liam raised his eyebrows.

Liam was thinking how ignorant the Westerners were about other religions. And in Jerusalem, the epicentre of the three great religions?

The last stop was the church of the Holy Sepulchre, sectioned off between various Christian sects. Liam broke off from the group to light a candle; to carry on the family tradition. They were role called by Moshe and left by Zion Gate.

The kibbutz had arranged for them to pay a visit to Yad Vashem, the Holocaust museum. When they drove to Mount Herzl, the Mount of Remembrance, a quietness came over the volunteers. Moshe told them that Yad meant memorial and Shem meant name. He led them down the Avenue of the Righteous among Nations. Amongst the many names Liam was looking for Mary Elmes from Cork who rescued hundreds of children from the Nazi's. And Hugh O'Flaherty, the pimpernel of the Vatican who defied the Nazis in Rome. He couldn't find their names among the vast array of nations honoured there. Only the name Oscar Schindler stood out like a beacon of bravery.

At the Children's Memorial to the million and a half who perished, a stunned silence ensued.

'When our children under the gallows wept,

The world it's silence kept.'

Liam saw Gunther wipe his face thinking it couldn't be easy for a German to confront. Before they left Moshe quoted from the book of Isiah:

'To them I will give within my temple and it's

walls a memorial and a name better than sons

and daughters.

I will give them an everlasting name that will

endure forever.'

In dribs and drabs, they boarded the bus for Bethlehem. It was less than six miles, but the early evening traffic was crawling. Mark remarked that they could run it faster to Gunther. Someone called out 'speak for yourself' and the sombre mood was lifted. As they entered the outskirts Moshe was pointing to a field on the left. Shepherd's Field but there were no flocks and no shepherd this Christmas Eve.

Manger Square was filling up with pilgrims as the bus pulled in. An Israeli soldier stepped in front of it, hand raised. Moshe was gesturing to the inside of the bus and pointing to the church. After a cursory glance inside they were waved forward.

The entrance to the Church of the Nativity was a bottleneck, a scrum. Liam queued with Mark and eventually picked their way down the narrow cave. Stable? There was a wrinkled face nun kneeling by a Latin inscription. A star at the centre with the lettering around it.

'Hic de Virgine Maria

Jesus Christus natus est'

Liam translated for Mark, reading round the circular text.
'Here is where Jesus Christ was born.'
When they were above ground again, they could hear the Palestinian choir singing. 'Adeste Fideles' ascended into the still evening air. Midnight Mass was by ticket only and a man was going around trying to sell them.

'Blimey, it's like Wembley on Cup Final day,' Mark declined the ticket.

They just had enough time for a falafel and coffee before heading back to HaOgen.

Only Jan and Gene worked on Christmas Day, the dairy and the kitchen. All the other volunteers got the day off but for the kibbutzniks it was just another working day. The day dragged; nothing new thought Liam. He started packing the clothes he wouldn't need for the remainder of his time. He had one last run with Mark, just the two of them. A long tradition they kept up over the years, working up an appetite for the Christmas dinner. He told Mark he would be meeting Sarah for dinner otherwise they would have the usual kibbutz meal. Mark remarked as they parted with a handshake: 'a kosher Christmas for you then.' He had to have his little joke; that was the English way!

After shaving carefully and showering he splashed on a generous spray of deodorant. It felt like he was going out on a date with the attendant butterflies fluttering around his stomach. He regretted not bringing a pair of slacks and jacket at least. He knew that Sarah would be dressed to the nines and he in jeans and tracksuit top.

Out on the balcony at seven he saw a car pass through the security gate. His heart gave a little leap, like a schoolboy at the Debs. Sarah wore a light green dress with a low bodice. Her fuller breasts pushed up and a necklace snug between them. Her oval face was lightly tanned, and she had a hint of eyeshadow. Her smiling lips were moistened with a shade of pink lipstick.

'Stunning,' he looked in her eyes as he got in the car.

The gold flecks sparkled like buttercups in fields of green.

'Thank you. Big effort for our last night out,' she turned the car.

'Me too,' he sent himself up.

'You're fine, smart enough for me.'

'Bet you never expected this.'

'Not in a millennium.'

'And you're wearing the colours?'

'Yes, in honour of my other country.'

Sarah had booked a table at the Bamboo restaurant on Sironit Beach. When they were seated Liam asked her about Cork, about home.

'Only my Mama left now, my Papa passed away a few years ago.'

'Did you make up before ...'

'A week before he passed, with Inbar and my Mama the peacemakers.'

'The second he saw his granddaughter he was smitten.'

'He seemed like a different person altogether; like my old Papa again.'

'My Mama used to tell him that he was putting dogma before his daughter, his only child. Now at the end it was the opposite. He reached out his hand to me, his breath catching. He whispered ' Mazel Tov, my daughter.''

With his other hand he touched Inbar on the cheek and smiled 'Yoffie' to her. Then with Mama we all saw him take his last breath, like a sigh.

Sarah was quiet for a moment as the wine was served. Liam was silent letting her talk like he was a conduit for her to unburden herself. She then told him about her father's early life in France. Hence her fluency in her first language.

How his parents were deported from Rivesaltes camp in Vichy France. Barely in his teens he watched the train pull away with the screams of his mother echoing in the empty platform. His father waving to him as if he were just going on a journey. But this was a permanent parting; there were no return tickets from Auschwitz. While still on the platform a woman came running up and dragged him away. He was tall for his age and looked old enough to work.

He was bundled into the boot of a car with another younger child. When it stopped, they were helped out by the woman he got to know as Mary. There was a makeshift camp there where he was given food and winter clothing. It was cold even in the foothills of the Pyrenees. He eventually ended up in Ireland, in the city of Mary Elmes. He was fostered in Albert Road, Cork, until he was old enough to start work. Ten years after losing his family he married his foster parent's daughter, replacing his lost family.

Liam could tell that she was still grieving for the father she had known. Without a word he got up and moved to the back of her chair. With his arms around her shoulders, he lay his cheek against her hair. No words were spoken, and he kissed her cheek and returned to his seat. The main course was served, no turkey this year. A kosher Christmas indeed. Sarah was trying to apologise for what she told him, but Liam said it made you understand your father better. She raised her glass and wished him a Happy Christmas. 'And Happy New Year while we're at it,' he answered.

'Your turn, what about you?'

'Like you, just my Mam at home.'

'My father was ...died a good few years ago.'

'My sister Aine is married to a bank manager in Dublin now. They have a son so I'm an uncle at least.'

'And marriage for you?' Sarah probed.

'Nowhere near,' he kept it light.

'Any girlfriends?' she arched her eyebrows.

'Not too many; I'm still running.'

Liam then told her about Marion, calling her his platonic pal. But after one of the demos, he found out that she had a girlfriend, Mona. They were sitting around drinking Aussie wine and listening to Bob Marley. When 'No Woman No Cry ' played Liam remarked 'that's me then.' Marion and Mona exchanged a look and laughed. Liam had totally missed the message contained there. In the morning when he nipped up to the bathroom he literally ran into Mona. This beautiful black girl was coming out of Marion's bedroom. Liam was first person that Marion came out to and they remained friends.

Then Liam told Sarah about Roxy who thought she was the athletes equivalent of the golf widow.

'I was only a notch on her bedpost. She had a thing about sportsmen, and I lost her to a footballer,' he finished wryly.

'So, I'm two nil down at the moment.'

'But first you picked a Jewish girl you thought went to Mass.' Sarah's eyes were twinkling.

'That's my hat trick then,' they were both laughing.

Sarah became serious suddenly, reaching across and taking his hand. He wondered what brought that on.

'Listen Liam, you know by now how much you mean to me.' I hope I mean the same to you. But my life is in Israel now with Inbar.'

'And you have made your own life in England.'

'Both of us in exile; a long way from where we met.'

'Even if our religions could reconcile or our cultures coalesce, we would still be apart.'

'So please Liam find yourself a good woman and settle down,' she squeezed his hand and let go.

'I suppose you're right; we must be realistic however hard.'

'I know I will never meet another that would mean as much as you.'

'First love is the deepest as the song goes.'

'But I'm going to miss you so much,' he took her hand back.

After fruit cocktails they lingered over coffee, reluctant for the night to end. Prolonging the parting that they knew was imminent. They knew in their hearts that the next goodbye was forever. So long. Before they left Sarah gave him a packet wrapped in coloured paper.

'Happy Christmas.'

'Thanks, you shouldn't have.'

'I'm sorry I didn't get you any present.'

'I thought...'

'You're right, it's not in our tradition.'

'Passover is.'

'But Sarah, there is something I'd like you to take for Inbar.'

'When you tell her about us would you buy her a necklace or pendant for her eighteenth birthday?'

'Please,' he implored as Sarah hesitated.

'It's important to me.'

'The very least I can do for my daughter, for you.'

'You really don't have to do anything but if you wish...'

'It's very thoughtful and kind of you anyway.'

'I'm pretty sure she will treasure it.'

'Perhaps an emerald pendant, a reminder of her roots,'

Liam reached for his wallet and pulled out his last hundred-dollar bill. That was the currency he was advised by the bank to take to Israel. He could see that Sarah was still unsure, but he wrapped it in her hand.

Back in Mishmar Liam sat on the sofa while Sarah made more coffee. Sitting together they were hesitant with each other. When they put their cups down, he reached across and kissed her cheek. She was turning in his hands, her eyes locked to his. Green into blue with the gold highlighting the hurt. Then her moist mouth was opening under his lips. He could feel the fullness of her breasts as they held each other.

They drew apart when they heard the door burst open. Inbar entered in her basketball top and shorts. She kissed her mother and said 'Shalom' to Liam. He was looking in her eyes, pale blue, his family trait.

Had Inbar seen them embracing? He got up to go, felt in the way of Sarah and her daughter.

' I have an early start for my last day.'

'Back to Pardes; I'll never eat another Jaffa again.'

Sarah put a wraparound across her shoulders. He held his hand out to Inbar. Her pale blue eyes reflected in his. Instead of taking his hand she brushed her lips like butterfly wings across his cheek. He hugged her slight body briefly. Over her shoulder Sarah was watching them intently. Father and daughter. Was she thinking ... like a family?

They were silent on the short drive to HaOgen. She stopped outside the security hut. Wordlessly, they held each other. He could see the guard watching them over her shoulder. The lamp in the hut catching a tear like a silver star falling.

'I'm going to miss you so much,' her voice muffled against his chest.

'Love you forever Sarah,' his throat caught.

Her lips against his cheek, wet where her tear had landed.

'So long,' she whispered, again.

'Shalom, shalom,' in unison.

They reluctantly let go, then a final hug and she was gone. He watched her turn the car around with a final wave. The sky was emptying a raincloud as the taillight flickered out at the end of HaOgen Road.

It was over. He knew. He nodded to the guard and walked slowly into the cold rain. Incongruously, he thought of a sentence from Chinua Achebe novel or short story. Was it 'Things Fall Apart? He couldn't say but it remained with him when he had forgotten the rest of the story.

'There were things like tears in his eyes'

A pathetic fallacy for a numb night.

Jan was still up when he got to Shalom Shack. He'd been to Netanya too celebrating a Swedish Christmas. Steak and Gold Star beer. He was half soft and insisted that Liam share a can of Maccabee with him. It was his last day working in the dairy.

'Christmas Day, Liam, working'! It was a day of goodbyes Liam thought taking a swig. They shook hands before going to bed as Jan was heading off at six next morning.

Pardes passed slowly going through the motions again. At four Liam took off his oversized clobber and threw it on Jan's bed. The depleted group of runners headed around the trails of the orange for a token jog. Liam put his name down for the minibus to the airport in the morning. The dining hall had thinned out when they had their evening meal.

'The last supper,' Mark called it.

Liam said his final goodbyes: the Swedish girls, Gunther, Gene and finally Mark.

'Well done mate.'

'Quite an adventure for you.'

'See you back in Blighty.'

'Thanks for everything Mark; yes, it's been some experience,' they had a slight hug on parting.

Mark was staying on along with Gunther until the spring. He had one final goodbye to make and knocked on Offra's door. She was at her desk writing out the kibbutz certificate all volunteers received on leaving. The certificat d'appreciation was in Hebrew and French.

Pour avoir travaille et

partage avec nous notre

forme sur de vie au kiboutz

fondee sur la fraternite

et la paix--shalom.

He asked Offra to write down the English translation before he left.
Kibbutz Certificate:

'As a token of appreciation for having worked and shared with

us our kibbutz way of life based on brotherhood and peace--

Shalom.'

Offra formally shook his hand at the door half hugging his shoulder.

Liam packed the last few things putting his marathon medal in the dirty gear at the bottom. Sleep was slow in coming; he had a knot like pain in his stomach. He was awake long before six his mouth furry and his eyes aching. He half missed Shalom Shack as he banged the door for the last time. He developed a raging headache from the clitter on the bus. A jumble of Scandi accents babbling away thirteen to the dozen. He didn't want to speak to anyone, drawing into himself. He gave the driver his last few shekels as a tip. The Swedish girls smiled goodbye to him as he entered the concourse. Shuffling through security he was asked to open his case. The x-ray had found his marathon medal in a dirty sock. He thought he saw the officials nose twitch but perhaps he nearly smiled. El Al: safe as houses!

On board at last, it was like a rugby scrum in the aisle. What a palaver he thought fighting his way to his seat. From his window seat he could see the sun sweeping across the tarmac. He had a fluttering feeling in his stomach on take-off. His heart was hollowed out knowing he would never see his Sarah again. When the plane was horizontal, he unwrapped her gift, guessing it would be a book.

'Where the Jackals Howl,' By Amos Oz, himself a kibbutznik. Inside the front flap was a gift card and an inscription. When he read the words she had written he had to blink his eyes towards the window. She had added the address of Mishmar Ha Sharon, postcode 1027000 included. Finally, the telephone number of the Ulpan. Before signing it, the first time he knew her full name. Sarah Goldstein. Before placing the book hemmed in by the window, he read the words again.

'Ever has it been

that love knows

not its own depth

until the hour

of separation.'

Kahlil Gibran

Lebanese poet

PART THREE

'Now I possess ... something else, called soul.

I am told that the soul never dies, is always

searching

and searching.

... Instead of succumbing to my homesickness,

I have told myself that my home is

everywhere.

Vincent Van Gogh

After a weekend of abject misery Liam dreaded going back to the office. It felt strange being on his own after the community of the kibbutz. He called Jamie but he was on duty over the weekend. He missed Mark and their long run on Sunday followed by a few pints in the White Horse.

His landlady had left a message on his bedside table with a telephone number to ring. Not recognising the London number, he left it until Sunday night. It wasn't Aunt Una or Marion and when he rang a faintly familiar voice answered. The musical tones of Mona with bad news about Marion. Cancer.

On Monday he was called into the Chief Executive Officer's suite. After congratulating him on the marathon he told him that the Civil Service magazine, 'Touchline', wanted to do a feature. But the editor of the sports page wanted a description of the race. What it was like to run a marathon in his own words. Liam told the Chief that he had an entry in his athletic diary that might do. But it needed to be typed or they wouldn't understand a word.

'I'll get Petra to type it if you fetch it in tomorrow.'

He was referring to the new personal assistant he had hired while Liam was away.

'And Liam before you go, I want to put your name forward for promotion, a new challenge, what?' If you can run a marathon, surely you are capable of running a department,' he smiled which was rare.

When Liam left, he met Petra at the door; 'good timing' the chief called out and introduced them. On his lunchtime run he jogged back to the digs for the diary. When he had showered at the Youth Club, he met Petra on her way back from lunch. He told her what 'his nibs' as the Chief was known had said. Handing her the diary he joked no official secrets in it but mind my scrawl.

When the reporter arrived in Friday Liam had to tog out and pretend to run in Priory park for privacy. Liam was thinking what if I'd won? The Times!

When the next edition came out, he was famous for a week. Late in the afternoon Roxy stopped as she was passing his desk. He was intent on keeping his head down, but she tapped him on the shoulder.

'Congrats on the marathon.'

'Bit of a racy photo in the mag as well,' he caught her smirk on looking up.

Tight top, short skirt in winter. Roxy to a tee.

'We should have a drink to celebrate.'

'Even for old time's sake,' she was serious.

'What about the footballer?'

'Out of action presently.'

'Apparently an overuse injury.'

'Not surprised with you.'

'Which leg; the middle one?'

'As well as his hammy as he calls it,' she started to move on.

'See you around.'

'Cheers anyway,'

When promotion came his way in the Spring he started to save for a mortgage. Every weekend looking at the prices in estate agents' windows. He narrowed the location down to the two parks in town.

After the diary entry was published people said he had a way with words. They said it was like a short story. Very, Liam thought. After his evening run, he started to dabble in writing. A boyhood Christmas scene. A child trying to make sense of the Troubles. Innocence hounded by race hatred.

'Colours': his first short story came to him while watching a documentary on TV.

He wondered would Petra do any private typing at home. It took him a long time before he approached her. He had noticed how quietly she went about her work. Never indulging in office gossip or going on the traditional Friday lunchtime drinks. He would notice her reading a book during her tea breaks which he took to be a good sign. He broached the subject in the canteen while she was sitting on her own. She said 'yes' straight away saying she enjoyed typing the piece for the magazine. She quietly insisted on doing it as a favour. He thought about inviting her to one of their Sunday nights at the White Horse. Then as his birthday was coming up decided on dinner.

'What if I buy you dinner instead?' My birthday is Saturday so if you're free?'

'That will be lovely. I shall have the typing finished by then.'

'Great, it's a date, sort of.''

Petra smiled her acceptance and Liam's life took a new turn.

He booked Oscars near the seafront. I suppose he thought later it was a 'small talk' meal. He learned she was a Londoner who had made 'Alia' to Essex in her teens. That she lived with her widowed mother and had a sister.

Over a couple of Irish coffees after the meal she handed him the typed story wrapped in a clear wallet. He speed read the six-page story, no typos in the text.

COLOURS

I was hungry and lost in London town. Putting an extra injection of pace into my walk, in a hurry to find the station. The rain that was menacing the sky moved closer. It fell, divided into wind splattered spits. A continuous attack that made the ground shine on my downcast face. Now and then a squall blew out from a side street to hold the sleet up to the streetlight. It was just like the beam of a film projector.

I tried to cross the wide street; no pedestrian crossing visible. A black cab screeched in front of me. It was like that scene from Midnight Cowboy. Only the driver was Ratso! Raising my head, meeting the cold glance of a passing girl. Eying her small breasts sogging through her summer dress. I threw a look to the end of the street. There was only one dim figure in the distance., a blur of blue.

'Excuse me Officer but how do I get to Charing Cross?'

The policeman gave me a 'gawd are you making them still' look and pointed across the street.

'You got it there, sir,' said without undue sarcasm.

'Thanks, are there any cafes nearby.'

'I,' the cop paused, 'I'm not in advertising you know.'

'I don't know; I thought you were touting for tyrants.'

Before the officer could recover his dignity, I was halfway across the street. Because it was quiet, I heard him remark under his breath.

'Red cheek.'

I didn't look back but put a hand to my cheeks. They were a moist silver. Commie backchat? That's it I figured and smiled to myself. About time the bobby became aware of the body politic.

Entering the cafe In Seine eight pairs of eyes got up from their plates. I felt rather than saw the bored beam. I didn't pursue any interest in the people present. They were busy mulling over teacups in various stages of deflation. Someone suddenly reached the bottom of a glass. Leather jacket and oily forehead jerked back from the relieved glass. I watched the jerk exchange a double bored look with his girlfriend. It seemed to say: Now that I've finished that wet chore, what next? Repeat! The girl dropped her lank hair across her eyes and committed her mind to a pale straw. The glass emptied along with her mind. It sounded like a second full stop in a short sentence.

I tried to hail the eye of the waitress; impossible, as she was cross-eyed. The biker picked up my gaze, but his eyes fell away when I gave him the full glint. Even numbers being his mathematical hang-up. Eventually, the waitress consented to come over. Her cheap biro pen poised like a weapon. Not mass destruction!

'Breakfast please,' I indicated the menu.

'Blimey breakfast,' she looked at her watch.

'No, just bacon and eggs,' I answered brightly.

'It's half two,' she raised her nasal voice.

'Thanks for the time,' I humoured her.

She flounced off, muttering to an indifferent audience.

'Brekkie at this time of day; well, I ask ye.'

I wished her success with the answer and looked ahead. The two rockers were stooping awkwardly from their table. The girl had a rumpled look, lack of sleep and less of soap. The mechanical faced youth looked in as they passed the rain draped window. It was falling in broken lines like silver ink on a moving page.

The waitress returned with a cup of dark brown tea. I was just about to risk a sup when I heard a carnival commotion outside. Looking sideways I noticed three couples exchange glances. A grim, grey pair preparing worried questions for a singular answer. One floral air designed the smile of knowing between them. The third pair, a couple of old dears gave a sullen grimace to each other. I was glad I wasn't a pair.

I tried a thick mouthful of tea and listened with the cafe. I half guessed it was some kind of demonstration. They were weekly events that crowds went to like a football match. I couldn't be solidly sure not having read anything about it. I could make out the ebb and flow of chanting. Imagining thousands of tongues coldly peppered against the grain of the wind. I picked out 'Ho' from the jumble. Can't be Vietnam; I'd been to enough of them to know. So 'ho' was not Chi Minh. Must have misheard, probably 'no'.

A worried visage hurried past my table. He was pointing a bunch of keys, like silver fingers. Locking the front door, he retreated through the animated customers. I was reminded of the Dutch dyke tale. The one about the boy not ...The transparency of the window was splintered by banners. To my sleepy eyes it was like a fantasy dawn. As if a century of rainbows looped across an endless sky. I felt the whole world go red with gold and black flags, for shine and shadow.

Even the banners seemed like the slow sweat of blood. I was affected for the first time that day by the violence of the vision. The expressions before my eyes were tight lipped and cold. Either the rain or the rage had paled their youth. With the water falling on their faces, they seemed to be weeping slowly.

Half turning, I saw a white coat appear at the corner of the window. A young black girl was leaning forward as if within the pane. From her outstretched hand a slow crack was bending across the glass. A red stain soaked the cuff of her raincoat. I reacted slowly in the languid day. I was mesmerised by the way the window was bending.

As she sprawled heavily on the corner table, I reached up to break her fall. I helped her to towards the leather wall seat. When I asked if she was ok, her head fell limp on her neck. I unbuttoned her bloody coat with one arm holding her upright.

'Ere, let me help you, man.'

I didn't look up; the Doc Martins introduced the voice. I briefly wondered did he follow her in by the window? The biker held her head up and I opened the coat fully.

'My window!'

'Is she alright?' the manager was looking from the window to the girl.

'She ain't half bloody left man,' the biker spat with venom.

'Somebody will pay for this,' the man spread his hands.

Somebody said 'yeah.'

The girl started to moan and shake her head.

'Water,' I ordered from the redundant waitress.

She strolled back as was her want and I held the glass to the girl's lips. The cold shock caused her to erupt from her stupor. A gush of diluted ice plunged down her neck. The first word she said was 'me?' At least she knows who she is I thought.

'Oh yes,' I fell in.

The pain slowly faded from her forehead.

'Thank to you,' she smiled brilliantly.

'Not at all,' I blushed in her warmth.

'I'd better try my legs.' she made to get up.

I held out an arm while she tested her strength.

'Fit.'

'I guess, thanks.'

'Well, I have a tube to catch,' I helped her up.

'I'm beginning to think we're characters from 24 Charing Cross Station,' she freed my arm.

'Well, that's where I'm bound for anyway. I didn't know it was numbered,' I added.

She gave me a puzzled look and laughed as if I'd cracked a joke.

'May I walk there with you then,' she linked my arm.

'Sure, no bother.'

We moved together to the now open door. I threw a couple of bob for the tea and a tip. The bikers waved a couple of limp hands. The manager was at the door before us, keys poised. Fingers of silver waving us goodbye.

Outside the street had fallen silent. A minute for the golden memory of a son. Bleeding like Olympic embers. The embryo architect felled at a bus stop. The dreams of his youth quenched. For colour.

Strangers mourned for his memory. Silent, silver, eternal tears.

For innocence.

'Thanks a million, Petra!'

'That's improved a fair bit from my scrawl anyway.'

'Not at all; I enjoyed typing it. Made a change from Civil Service speak,' she smiled her shy smile.

'You should try to get it published, perhaps in a literary magazine.'

'Not sure it's that good,' he replied modestly.

'Do you mind if I ask you. Was it about someone specific?

'Yes and no; but it could be about any victim of racism.'

'Didn't he want to be architect? '

'That was his dream.'

'Wasn't he also an athlete like you,' Petra smiled, a glint in the candlelight.

'Anyway, his proud white killers were neither.'

'Just architects of evil.'

Liam went on to tell Petra about his visit to the Holocaust museum in Jerusalem.

'Well, in Israel I saw where racism ultimately led.'

'The evidence of evil proven in Yad Vashem.'

'Think it means monument and name.'

He repeated the quotation Moshe had recited at Yad Vashem.

'I will give them in my house and within my walls a monument and a name which shall not perish,'

'And on that sombre note ...' he finished.

'Yes, thanks for a lovely evening,' she was reaching for her purse.

'I can see that Israel had an effect on you.'

Not half Liam was thinking.

'May I pay half?'

'No way, this is on me and thanks for the typing.'

'And the company on my birthday.'

'You can pay next time,' he left it up in the air.

'Yes, on my next birthday then.'

Liam paid the bill and she dropped him off at the digs. He wondered should he give her a peck on the cheek at least. But in the end, they shook hands. How old fashioned he thought as he waved her goodbye.

Mark returned from Israel at the end of April. He looked tanned and lean, like a fawn whippet as Jamie described him. On their first run Liam could barely keep pace with him. Jamie let them go calling out from behind 'what's the express'? Mark had gone up to a new level; his mileage was a minute faster even on the long runs. He attributed it to training with Gunther who was on the point of selection with the German national team. Before the season was out Mark had established himself as a serious competitor. International races followed and he made rapid progress. Of course, Jamie had to ask him what he was on. Moving up in distance and longer reps was the answer. The speed he developed over 1500m was now a potent weapon over 5k.

When Liam saw Mark on his own during their lunchtime five, he asked him if he had seen Sarah since. He replied cagily that he thought he saw her with Gene in Netanya one Shabbat. Apparently, Gene had left HaOgen shortly after Liam had left. Once he sorted his business in America he returned as a kibbutznik. Mark had heard he was attending the Ulpan in Netanya for lessons in Hebrew. Liam knew Sarah was working there part time. He felt a pang of jealously not unlike when he first heard about Haim. What did he expect? He knew Sarah could never be his. And yet ...

He asked Petra out again to the runners' night in the White Horse. Was he on the rebound he wondered? Finally facing up to reality. Petra was very quiet in company until Jamie brought her out of her shell. He definitely had a way with words and women. Liam noticed how her eyes softened when she first saw the Birdie boy. A name Jamie came up with to make her smile. He might also have given Derek the Dust his moniker when he found out he was a refuse collector for the council.

Mark won his first British vest in September. He beat a French world champion after a titanic battle over 5k. Even though it was a road race his time was just off the Olympic qualifying time. On a tartan track that would be upgraded. Jamie wondered would he still want to train with 'us pedestrians' but he always did. He would let Liam and Jamie set the pace on the long runs. Mark called that training 'time on your feet'.

'Time off our feet,' Jamie joking, trying to keep pace.

The Civil Service sports club held its annual dinner dance every October. Liam put it to Mark it would be a good occasion to celebrate his elevation to elite runner. Mark was dubious as he didn't have anyone to ask. You could borrow one from Jamie's harem Liam suggested. Then more sensibly suggested he ask Fiona.

'After all, you are best buddies, related through drink.'

Petra said yes straight away, and Mark finally asked Fiona out. For Liam, the tricky bit came after the dinner when the disco started. As a child of the sixties, he wasn't au fait with the music. Mark became animated when the Undertones was played, 'Teenage Kicks'. Liam was saying 'bit past that' over the loud chorus. It was Fiona who got them on their feet when a slow one came on. Liam just shuffled around in Petra's arms. Mark and Fiona were locked in a smooch in their own world.

When 'A Good Heart' played the words struck a chord with Liam. It was Fiona who winked at him over Marks shoulder that did it. She was indicating Petra as the refrain a 'good heart is hard to find ' was repeated. Liam smiled at Fiona and did the same, nodding at Mark. It was Petra who noticed Fiona's fondness for Mark. A lovely couple she said with a question in her voice. Like us Liam thought?

Before the end of the year Liam had enough for a deposit on a mortgage. He settled on a one-bedroom flat in Southchurch with a balcony overlooking the park. Not Shalom Shack he thought back to the rickety balcony in HaOgen. No more pokey bedsits or digs dictated to by money mad landlords. Mark and Petra volunteered to help him decorate before moving in.

'Err on the side of generosity,' Mark entreated when they were pasting the wallpaper in the kitchen. Petra turned out to be a very good painter, especially the tricky corners. On a cold Saturday in November, he moved in; Petra driving his meagre possessions in the back seat and boot. The first time he had his own keys since leaving home.

Before the start of winter training Jamie suggested targeting a spring marathon. Liam had his doubts, the pain of Galilee still in his memory. Mark was of the view that the increase in milage would be a solid foundation either way. Liam was in when Mark said he'd draw up a schedule and pace all their twenty-mile runs. In January Jamie broke down, plagued by niggles and had to drop out of the schedule.

The first London marathon was advertised in Athletics Monthly and Liam entered just in case. He could hedge his bets if the training weren't going well. Mark ensured he was prepared this time. No cramp, no crawl. On a rainy day in London, he found himself lining up with over 6,000 other runners. He was on schedule for six-minute mileage at the Cutty Sark. The rhythm of the rain kept time with his cadence on the tarmac. When he reached Tower Bridge, he felt his confidence grow. Only in the Isle of Dogs did he encounter uncertainty.

He was floating along for twenty miles before the fuel started to run out. At twenty-two he thought he was going to hit the wall. But it was at Birdcage Walk that he hit the first blip. He ran carefully on the precarious cobbles. The extra mileage had paid off and he knocked twenty minutes off his time from the Sea of Galilee marathon.

When Mark met him at the finishing line Liam was in the head between the knees pose. On the return journey Mark was saying it was pity we're going to miss the White Horse. Liam was thinking it was nourishment he needed more than drink. He realised he hadn't eaten since breakfast if you'd call a banana breakfast. Mark had a Sunday roast to look forward to at home.

'I wish I had,' Liam had only yogurt in the fridge,
'Time you settled down, mate.'

'A roast and a roger!'

'What more do you need?'

'What about Petra?'

'She fancies the pants off you.'

'I could do worse I suppose,' Liam was half asleep, half listening.

'And what about that bird in Israel?'

'Sarah, innit?'

'Not realistic.'

'I guess, too old for the bar whatsit too.'

'Bar Mitzvah, Mark.'

By the summer, the kernel of the idea Mark had suggested had taken root. He invited Petra to London for Angie's First Communion with Aunt Una's approval. No doubt she would be telling his mother about Liam's girlfriend. He could imagine his mother saying, 'not before time.' After a night over in Una's they took a trip to the West End.

Petra wanted to visit a fading Carnaby Street, its heyday in the sixties just a memory. Mary Quant hairstyles and short skirts giving way to punk pink and maxis. Liam had a hankering to visit Abbey Road and walk the crossing that the Beatles made famous.

'I Wanna Hold Your Hand'.

They held hands for that first time in London; Petra slipping hers into his on the iconic crossing. He remembered how he wanted to hold Sarah's hand down Panna to the Lee. Just to see the Beatles in a Hard Day's Night. Another Saturday. He squeezed Petra's hand in guilt, and she just smiled.

Liam was due his annual leave in September and would be going home. Petra told him her family often took their holidays in the West Country or the Highlands of Scotland. Over a drink one weekend in the Parson's Barn, he asked her home. They were talking about holidays and he casually said, 'What about Ireland for a change?'

'Sounds lovely,' she smiled her agreement.

She later told him about her mother's concern. She had mistaken Kerry for Derry and thought they would be in a war zone. She wouldn't be the first Liam thought having heard such comments himself whenever a bomb went off. He had written another short story around the subject of the Troubles. He must remember to ask Petra to type it like she did 'Colours'.

They flew out from Stansted to Cork on a Ryan Air cheap and cheerful. Too late to catch the train to Kerry, they walked over Patrick's bridge from the bus station. Liam thought they might find a B&B in Wellington Road. Ardagh House welcomed them, and they took a twin-bedded room. After showering they strolled down from Patrick's Hill. In McCurtain Street they had a meal in another Oscars. They laughed at the coincidence; their first date.

Liam's mother was still living in the farmhouse although the land was now rented out for grazing. She made a fuss of Petra and Liam realised how alike they were in their quietude. His mother had prepared two rooms and Petra exchanged a smile with Liam. As he remarked later, 'we had to go with the holy flow!' His mother had prepared what she called high tea although Liam thought it was like any other supper he'd had.

After eating Liam took Petra into town in a hackney car his mother called for. They went to his father's old bar - the Corner House. The two old ladies who presided over it in his father's day were long gone. There was a ballad lounge there now unlike before when they would be impromptu singsongs. His father usually, like a lead singer in a group, a one-man band. It was there that Petra heard her favourite folk song 'The Cliffs of Dooneen.' Liam was reminded of Marion and her roots in Clare. His mother thinking, she was the one and he never told her why it couldn't be. Now Petra was firmly in the favourite position and he would not have the same excuse this time.

Petra's birthday was coming up during the holiday and his mother baked a cake. Liam bought her a cassette of Irish folk songs which included 'the Cliffs' of wherever it was. His mother insisted on taking her out to dinner. Liam booked a table in the Kingdom Hotel for the Saturday night.

When they were leaving for town in a hackney car Petra turned back.

'What's up?' Liam looked behind.

'You left the key in the lock,' Petra turned to his mother.

'That's grand; who'd rob us,' she linked Petra's arm to the car.

'Oh, alright,' Petra had a puzzled look on her face.

It would be unheard of by her own mother, a Londoner.

The two weeks flew by, the weather held. He took Petra to the places of his boyhood. She was a great one for walking and loved the wilderness of the woods. She would pick a selection of flowers, bluebells and buttercups. When she picked a bunch of yellow flowers and his mother saw it, she said she'd have to throw them out. Petra was crestfallen and when his mother told her that they were 'piss-a-beds' she was in stitches. They would hire bikes for the day and picnic in the shelter of the sand dunes in Whitestrand.

Liam showed her around their farm that was. The Upper Meadow gone to rough grass, only fit for bullocks. To think his father had spent years saving hay there. Petra was picking bog cotton along the slough as they made their way to the River Field. Liam looked into the dark clouded water looking for answers. How could you drown in such a shallow flow; it wasn't even a current. Petra linked his arm on the bank; she sensed something. But Liam was silent and turned her around to go back. Before they packed for the return journey his mother was hinting about settling down. After her hopes for Marion, she was praising Petra at every turn. And when Petra showed her how to make banana cake it clinched it. She called her a ' cordon blue' chef!

'You'd be well looked after,' she whispered to Liam.

'Next time you see us, who knows,' he told her on goodbye.

She hugged Petra for a long time reluctant to part. Liam could tell she was lonely on her own. She remained at the door waving them away until the hackney car had left the lane.

When they were away Liam missed Marks second international race in Valentia. This time he had to settle for second over 10k to a Spanish Olympian. After the race, the national coach talked to him and agreed to provide a schedule that would take him up to another level. Up to then Mark was self-coached, a voracious reader of training manuals. His gospel propagated by Percy Cerutty, the Australian coach. Long runs;

sand dunes and reps became the norm for Mark although he had to travel for the sand dunes. The long intervals were called repetitions after his coach told him reps were for insurance agents. Pedantic or what? as Jamie exclaimed in the White Horse. Once again Mark assured them that he would still train with them. But, at the risk of sounding repetitious no reps for me if you please, was Jamie's take on it.

By Christmas Liam had bought an engagement ring in a side street jeweller. On the Eve he booked a table in an Italian restaurant at the end of the High Street. It would be his last trip to London for Christmas. Over coffee he produced the tiny packet and casually said ' your Christmas present.' Petra in turn had a large packet by her side. As they exchanged gifts Petra started to put hers in her handbag. 'You better make sure it fits,' he started to open his.

'A Helly Hansen, thank you.' he half opened it to look inside.

Petra reached inside her bag and her eyes widened when she opened the packet.

When she put it on her ring finger she reached across and shyly kissed him.

'Now that it fits, I suppose we might as well get married,' he said coolly.

'You old romantic, you,' she twirled the ring round her finger.

'So, is that a, yes?' he raised a quizzical eyebrow.

'It is, I'd love to.'

They had a liquor to celebrate and held hands on the way to the car.

She drove him to the flat to collect his bag for the journey to Aunt Una's.

'Who knows, perhaps we'll have our own Christmas next year,' he hugged her before getting out.

'Let's hope so,' she leaned over and kissed him goodbye.

Aunt Una was delighted with the news, but Angie was upset that her 'Cousie' might not be visiting her for Christmas anymore. Una placated her by saying 'aren't you a little old for My Little Pony now'. They went to Midnight Mass as usual. This was Liam's once a year occasion to darken the door of a church. He was only a cultural Catholic now like Sarah to secular Judaism. On Christmas morning Una rang his mother and handed the phone to him. His mother was as relieved as delighted; she worried about him living on his own. Not for long more Mam he told her. He asked her to tell Aine and it was done.

A bleak start to the New Year with snow and ice. Liam had to get out the Helly Hansen for the freezing nights training. On the weekends he found it exhilarating running on newly fallen snow. You really had to work hard to get your legs out of the drifts. Even if he slipped, he wouldn't get injured, only his pride. In the short evenings he looked for something to read. There was only one book he had put off reading. He had hidden 'When Jackals Howl' away in his bedside table drawer. He couldn't face it after returning from Israel; he didn't know why. The night he retrieved it Sarah's gift card with her address fell from the flap. An omen, a reminder?

He decided to write to her to let her know he would be getting married. And Inbar? She would soon be old enough to do her National Service. Taking the oath 'Masada shall never fall again.' And the pendant? Did she have it and would she wear it when she was told the truth. He had a feeling of being on trial again. Ironically, he had just finished another short story and called it:

Adrian was also fifteen when he left school. The last day was spent without lessons. Instead, the maths teacher talked to the class about soccer. He suddenly changed the game to Gaelic when the Head entered.

A final word about behaviour during the long summer holidays; his pet subject being civics. Random murmuring as the door closed behind his black skirted back. A boy at the back shouting out in the ensuing silence.

'Aren't Manchester more a religion than the church to some people.'

Eyes turned to Adrian, half accusing, some pitying. He coloured under their long looks but tried to effect indifference.

'He's the same colour as their jerseys too.'

A skitter went up from the desk to his right. He didn't look up as the agricultural voice cracked the set of his face.

'Isn't his father a Commie? why wouldn't his face be red!

'The June sun lengthened across the classroom and he felt the heat multiply on his face. The teacher held up his hand and banged it on the front desk for attention.

'Now now boys, that's enough nonsense for now.'

'We've only got another hour so who's going to give us a song?'

'We already had the comedians,' he looked down to Adrian.

Someone whispered 'proper order'; was it Derry?

Brendy Brennan, the Civil Servant's son was shuffling to his feet.

'I do not know what song to sing,' he enunciated slowly.

'An Irish song of course, a coarse voice growled.

Brennan fingered his fáinne, the faded gold over his heart that proved he could speak Irish.

'What about a pop song instead?' Eddie his echo asked plaintively.

'Do you know a classic?' the neutral teacher asked.

'I know only one; O Solo Mio.'

'Or it's Now or Never, in English,' he explained.

'It's the same air,' he added helpfully.

'Jasus Christus,' a Latin scholar groaned, not wishing to sound profane.

'A solo what,' another voice piped up.

'Must be a solo run,' came the answer from the back desk.

'What class of football is that?' the first voice retorted.

A wave of giggles and guffaws swept over the class. When at last a semblance of silence prevailed Brennan began. Adrian listened to the words, a litany of loss and loneliness. When Brennan sang 'kiss me my darling' with a flat 'A' the whole class erupted in ridicule. Later as the clock wound down the day the class stood up for the Angelus. One more song and it was time to break up in a mad melee for the door.

Adrian walked slowly out the door, his satchel swinging idly by his side. Down the musty stairway, past the ancient portrait of Ignatius Rice. The playground a seething mass of bodies and bikes. At the gate he looked back at the faded yellow bordered by green railings. He felt strangely sad and turned fretting into freedom. He was jostled from his reverie by a playful shoulder.

'God but it's good to escape from Mountjoy,' Derry Daly fell in step with him.

'Hi Der, I suppose it's a bit like a prison alright,' Adrian conceded.

'I could have plugged holy Joe there; he had no right to open his insulting gob,' Derry's moon face was flushed.

'Ho Derry, goin' on the night shift for the holidays,' a voice shouted across the street.

'Ah, pull your wire, Willie,' Derry returned the barb.

'That's if you can see it, slob,' he added to the obese boy

'Aren't they a laugh, all women talk but they couldn't shift a mot.'

'Take plenty of no notice, Der,' Adrian dismissed the adolescent exchange.

'Let's cross the Rubicon, out of their way,' Adrian made a turn for the bridge.

'Suppose you'll be playing soccer for the summer?' Derry had a hint of hope in his voice.

'A little. I expect every fine evening anyway,' Adrian kicked a Players pack along the bridge.

'You must be flying fit,' Derry smiled.

'Um,' Adrian mused, 'aren't you?'

'Me? Fit to feint,' Derry made a balls of a body swerve.

'Well, that's GAA training for you; only fit for feck all,' Adrian bit his lip and quickly added, 'Will you be playing Gaelic yourself?'

'Ah no, I'd like to try my hand at the soccer this summer.' Derry was looking expectant.

'As a goalkeeper you mean?'

'Crikey no, I...' Derry hesitated at Adrian's raised eyebrow.

'Ah bother, I see what you mean.'

'No hands, of course,' Derry laughed at himself.

'You can train with me in the lawn,' Adrian offered.

Derry kicked a stone in delight before grimacing.

'You're a brick, Adrian.'

'I'm one hard man alright,' Adrian gave a little shoulder shove.

They parted at the end of the bridge, slapping each other on the back like teammates. Derry swung his schoolbag behind his back and sauntered down the quay.

'See you at seven so,' Derry called back.

'Fine, fellow, good luck,' Adrian took the bridge that led out of town.

The tide had ebbed on the river; a silhouette of the hill skimmed the shore. Beyond the bridge the distant Drum Hills were tinged with the gold of furze. The whitewashed walls of the farmhouse shone against the green of the fields.

Adrian threw his satchel into the corner between the dresser and the television. His mother must be in town, so he foraged in the fridge for a lump of cheese. He cut a slice of shop bread and made an excuse for a sandwich. Upstairs, he doused his hot face in cold water. A cool breeze fanned his face as he opened the bathroom window. The sky was blazing blue in a heat haze. The breeze brushed the grass along the Front Meadow. He stood gazing at the ring of gold furze on the back hill. When he went back down, his mother was in the hall managing the messages.

'Where were you Mam? I'm starving.'

'In town getting a few grudles for the supper. I see ye're all let loose from school early. 'You'll be gadding all over the globe now I suppose.'

'Not today anyway, I'm too weak with the hunger.'

'Oh, you poor pet.'

'Have a cup of that with a slice of bread an' sugar,' she lobbed a bottle of milk into his lap.

'Lunch will be ready in a jiffy; I'm gasping for a brew myself.'

'Righto.'

His mother buttered a crust for him, and he gulped the milk down.

'Any letter?' he was glad his mother was in the scullery.

The question fell from him and hung in the air. In the pause he was about to repeat himself when the answer came.

'Not a line.'

'The post is slow … maybe tomorrow?'

'Mam, do you think I'll ever get to Manchester?'

'Adrian,' his mother came to the scullery door, wiping her eyes. 'Onions,' she explained as a shadow crossed his face.

'You and your Manchester United! You can't live on dreams,' she chided.

'Dad did, does…' he trailed off

He saw a deep sorrow cross her brow, furrowed like a ploughed field.

'Like father, like son,' she said to herself.

'No Adrian, you're too bright to waste your life chasing a football.'

'God knows, your father...'

'He doesn't. God doesn't know Dad,' he cut in, a hard edge to his voice.

'Has someone said anything to you?' His mother sat next to him on the kitchen settle.

'What's a Commie, Mam?'

'A Communist you mean,' she didn't laugh.

'That's a lie anyway,' she continued.

'He's a Socialist; that means he believes that nobody should profit from another man's labours.'

'There's more to it than that but it's too complicated for me to explain.'

'What do you call that soccer team of yours?'

'Man United, why?' Adrian was puzzled.

'Because that's your father's faith. Man United, but with a small m,' she smiled sadly.

The smile faded from her face as she asked.

'Did someone say he was a communist so?'

'Yes, a commie, in the classroom.'

'They all laughed, except Derry.'

'What did the teacher say?'

'Nothing,' Adrian said flatly.

'I'll give him 'nothing.''

'We'll put a stop to that the first day you go back.'

'I'm not,' he said quickly.

'Not? What does that mean?'

'I'm just not going back to school.'

'But you have to. What else are you going to do?'

'I don't know,' he walked to the window.

Looking at the pristine paddock he whispered, 'go to Manchester.'

'But Adrian you're only fifteen.'

'You wouldn't get to Dublin on your own,' she was by his side.

'I can't go back Mam,' he said with conviction.

'Listen boy, there's a long way to go yet.'

'We've all the time in the world to talk it over.'

'How about it, right?'

'Alright,' he agreed reluctantly.

Knowing he would never walk through that green gate again.

Summer pondered over the borderland. The fields partitioned by the river grew gold with hay. His father should be here for harvest time. Instead, a bachelor farmer helped draw the wynds home to the haggard.

The evenings were drawing out over the Lawn as Adrian and Derry practised. Dreaming in the dark green night. The pals were as constant as the summer season. Cycling to the strand during the heat of the day. Diving off the rocks and swimming to the far shore. Running up sand dunes to strengthen their legs. Skinning down tall cliffs for balance.

Evenings began at seven and ended when the white ball blurred in the gathering dusk. Light diminishing imperceptibly in early September. The last Sunday evening of the holidays rained. Darkness came early with the change; Autumn imminent at eight. Adrian got up to pull the curtains when he couldn't read the Sunday Independent anymore.

'It's over,' he said looking out at the drenching land. A flood had gathered at the horses well and flowed down the Front Field. Behind the house the hill huddled, hidden by the night.

'May's well say bye to summer for another year,' his mother pulled the curtain properly.

'Well Adrian, how about it Tuesday?' she said out of the blue.

'I don't know if I can face it Mam.'

'If I got a job until Dad writes,' Adrian finished lamely.

'Live horse and you'll get grass,' she came out with an old saying.

'Until Christmas so,' he conceded.

'Everyone writes at Christmas,' he said without belief.

'We'll see,' his relieved mother went to prepare their supper.

On Monday, his mother was calling at his bedroom door. She was waving something in the air when he called 'come in.'

'What's the time?' he mumbled into the sheet.

'Eleven, look what I have?'

'A letter, a letter!' he copped on.

'Is it from Manchester, Mam?'

'No Adrian,' she opened the flap.

His face fell; he shrugged his shoulders.

'But Adrian, he's coming home.'

His face lit up slowly and he cautiously asked 'when?'

'Tomorrow,' she watched his eyes awake.

'Tomorrow,' he repeated quietly, without belief.

The Angelus bell rang out as he crossed the bridge. The tide seemed to ebb and flow with the sound. Derry's mother answered his knock; her frame filled the doorway.

'Ah, it's the soccer star.'

'My foot,' he riposted. 'Is Der up yet?' He wondered how he going to squeeze past her.

'Only just beat the bell,' she meant the Angelus. 'He's lunching with his breakfast. Here, come in,' she let him edge in.

Derry was in the kitchen, wiping egg from his mouth.

'How's Derry?'

'Hi Adrian.'

'Have we another week off? Your face is bursting!'

'What is it, a plague?'

'No such luck.'

'My Dad is on his way home.'

Adrian whispered in case Mrs Daly was listening. She was well known in town as the Daly News!

'Jeeze, that's great news; so, you'll be going back after all.'

'Unless there's that plague you were praying for,' Adrian laughed.

The short day flew over the Lawn; they had a goal-to-goal match that Derry won. You may think it was the cup final the way he celebrated; half jumping in the air. Clouds hovered over the horizon as they blew the final whistle on their freedom. A breeze sent the rain scuttling down the back hill. After parting in haste Adrien sprinted over the bridge on strong summer legs.

After high tea Adrian took the TV page from the Independent to see what was on.

'Anything worth watching?' his mother was dozing by the Stanley.

'Only the news, in ten minutes.'

'There won't be much good in that either,' she yawned.

'Good evening, here is the news, first the headlines.'

The blonde-haired woman was reading, enouncing every word. His mother went to the scullery to make the cocoa.

'Anything strange on the western front,' she held out his mug.

'Two shot in Derry'.

'It's a fright altogether. Soldiers?'

178

'No, a boy of sixteen and a woman standing in her own doorway.'

'The boy is dead and the woman lost an eye.'

'Plastic bullets?'

'A British army spokesman said the boy was wielding a Hurley.'

'The weapon, the army said he was carrying has not been found.'

'It was too, found my foot,' his mother drained her cup.

'The woman had just retrieved a milk bottle from the doorway.' Another weapon?

'Are you ready for a re-fill.'

'Nearly,'

Adrian was thinking of Derry's name, the same as the sundered city. The news was almost over, just the incidental regionals. The reader paused: a late news flash. Adrian sipped a second cocoa, half listening.

'At Heathrow Airport two men were arrested as they were about to board a flight to Dublin.'

The accused, one said to be from the North and the other the Republic were later charged with planting an incendiary device in an Underground station.

'Here is a report from our London correspondent.'

'The men named as Martin McAllister, 24 of Londonderry and Adrian Dowling...

His mother gripped his shoulder, her other hand to her mouth. Adrian felt a shiver sweep over him. In cold silence they listened to the smooth words.

'... stated to be members of a breakaway group of the Provisional IRA, Saor Eire. The device exploded during the end of the rush hour, leaving 19 people injured, 4 seriously.

McAllister, a teacher refused to recognise the court, in a special sitting. Dowling a self-educated Marxist who left school at fifteen claimed he was in Manchester at the time of the explosion. A starting pistol was found in his holdall wrapped in a red football jersey.

'The latest headlines.'

'The ceasefire is over.'

'That's the end of the news.'

'The utter end, the future's not worth a prayer,' his mother's hand was still locked to his shoulder.

A cold weight lifted from his body and blinding water swam before his eyes. Through a film he saw his father resting his hands on his shoulders and promising.

'Upon my word Adrian, I'll go to Manchester and see the Manager himself, if needs be.'

'Practice every day especially your right leg,' his father smiled. A left footer Adrian only used his right for standing on.

'God knows, a boy needs to dream, just as a man does.'

'Life puts us all on trial and if I can pull it off, you'll get your chance.'

'A trial at Old Trafford.'

They were his father's last words before he left.

'So, that's the trial he gave you, a fine legacy for his only son.'

A dark and bitter edge rent his mother's voice as she sat, immobile, staring at the screen.

'I want to see that letter, Mam.'

Silently, his mother went to the dresser, fumbling in the drawer.

'Here you are, his broken will.'

She saw the hurt in his hunched shoulders.

'Never mind me Adrian, it's only my heart that's scalded.'

Adrian opened the loose flap and lifted the letter out. He read the Kilburn address and stopped dead. Without reading a line he folded the letter and pushed it back in the envelope. Standing in front of the dresser he turned the envelope over. The Queen's head was blurred by a black halo. He idly read round the postmark: the time, the date ...Manchester.

'Mam, look, Manchester!'

He held up the letter like he'd scored a goal for Man U.

'Look, it was posted in Manchester.'

Together they stared at the letter, at the screen where the news had passed on. At each other.

Manchester?

The questions were piling up in his mind. Was he ambivalent about the Troubles? 'The rituals of revenge,' as he had said to Sarah so long ago. The denouement: innocent or guilty? Black and white with no grey to balance. He was part of a suspect people in England. To make light of it he would say 'it's called 'sleeping with the enemy' referring to himself and Petra. When she typed it over a weekend, they didn't have a similar discussion as they had over 'Colours'. The same with Mark and Jamie; Ireland was taboo. All the bombs and the bullets went over their heads. Running was their religion, and they left the politics to Jamie.

Liam's next trial was how to tell Sarah that he was getting married. He wondered how he would feel if it was the other way around. He only got as far as writing Sarah's address in Mishmar Ha Sharon. How to address her, formal or friendly?

He waited for the weekend before going back to the blank page. He would thank her again for the time they spent in Netanya. And especially the magical day cycling around the Sea of Galilee. The memory of her sun gold hair flying away behind her flushed face. And later after the trauma of Yom Kippur sleeping side by side for the first and last time. As pure and platonic as sister and brother. Thank her again for the Amos Oz and the pertinent inscription by Khalil Gibran.

Dear Sarah,

Hello again.

Shalom to Inbar.

Hope you are both well in Mishmar, ever get back to HaOgen? Mark thought he saw you once in Netanya before he returned to what he calls 'Blighty'! Any account of Gene? If you see him tell him I said 'hi.' No jokes now!

I'm really writing to let you know that I'm taking your advice. Petra is her name, the same as the rose red city in Jordan. We are due to be married in September. Mark will be my best man as well as my best buddy.

How about you? I used to fear that we'd marry strangers. I suppose we have to be realistic. Not magic realism? Life doesn't always move in linear lines. There are cross-roads; decisions on what tangents to take. I know I'm being too serious as usual, like the first day we met. You had your own word for our teenage angst: existential! Time to grow up.

I wonder did you buy that pendant for Inbar? If so, I hope it brings her luck when she starts her National Service. You must be so proud of her serving her country, yours too now. 'Daughter of Israel'?' It must be imminent as she approaches her eighteenth. Also, I hope she can understand what happened between us.

Thanks again for the wonderful time we spent, so fleetingly. And especially that day and night in Galilee. What a special place; I can never forget it.

I'm just about to read the Amos Oz novel ' Where Jackals Howl'. That inscription with those poignant words was heart-breaking, and beautiful.

Like you Sarah.

'So long again.'

And Sarah, you're often in my thoughts and always in my heart.

Shalom,

Liam

Liam's form deserted him over the track season. Only once did he come anywhere near four minutes for the 1500m. A frustrating five seconds short in the same race as Mark who shattered his personal best; 3.49. Jamie opted for the 5k and by virtue of the fact it was his first also a PB. On the way back from Cambridge he was teasing Mark with 'his first-class honours' from the university city. There was talk in the club that he could be its first Olympian. The coach had geared his training to moving up a distance. The 1500m was merely a speed session. The longer reps were paying off as his times tumbled close to the Olympic qualifying time for 5k. Los Angeles was on the horizon.

With the approach of the wedding, Petra and Liam were busy with the arrangements It would be a modest affair with scarcely fifty attending. He could feel his running suffering; not half as much as to come according to Jamie. 'A bourgeois construct,' he called marriage. The dictatorship of the proletariat.

'Cor blimey,' you have Marx as your bible.'

'Everything is ideology with you.'

'I'd nearly swear to God if I believed,' Mark said a mouthful.

Liam was thinking those two would start an argument in a telephone booth. And yet, the best of friends behind it all.

It was a semi-Catholic service; Liam didn't want to upset his family. Once a Catholic and all that. Petra didn't mind; she hadn't been to church since she was a child. Sunday school and Christmas. They often passed the church she was nearest to - St. Lawrence Church of England - but she didn't even suggest it.

In the end after driving around the boundary of the borough they found a church in her parish.

When they knocked on the door adjoining the church, they discovered that the priest was from Galway. He agreed to marry them in his church and took them through the routine. He made no attempt to convert Petra as Liam had worried about. He was thinking he'd have his work cut out with him to begin with. Liam admitted he wasn't very devout himself. More of a 'cultural Catholic' he told the priest.

'I haven't heard that one before,' the priest smiled.

A new excuse for the a la carte Catholics! They spent a fair amount of time talking about sport. Liam had been wearing his club tracksuit with the name emblazoned across the back. The priest had played rugby with Connaught in his younger days.

On the way home after the first meeting Liam was reassuring Petra.

'At least he didn't try to convert you to Rome.'

'Why, did you think he might,' Petra was all serious.

'Well, he is an ex-rugby player,'

'He'd have a job'!

They burst out laughing at the image.

The track season had more or less ended for Liam. Mark and Jamie had a few more open meeting races while Liam opted out. Petra wanted to have a small dinner party before the wedding with just a handful of their close friends. They had the 'soiree ' as Jamie called it in Liam's flat. They asked Mark and Fiona. Unusually, Jamie didn't have a current girlfriend, so Liam asked Roxy to balance the group. The footballer was up North for a league match. He hadn't fancied Crewe on a freezing cold night. The Southern softie Roxy called him when he tried to fake a hamstring tweak. His physio was a Geordie and didn't buy it.

They all brought presents for Petra; Liam had a Claddagh ring wrapped in readiness. Fiona brought a necklace with a thistle motif while Mark had a pendant of an English rose. Roxy brought an ornament of Spion Kop with 'You'll never walk Alone ' in gold lettering on it.

'Very 'appropriate,' Petra, a Spurs fan, hugged her diplomatically. And Jamie, being Jamie brought a wooden carving of a hammer and sickle. Luckily, the symbolism was lost on all but Liam. Mark asked Jamie didn't he have a Leek for the full set and Jamie replied, 'I did before I came out, thanks.'

Liam bought the wine, Jacobs Creek and a Chardonnay from the Clare Valley. Petra did the cooking, braised steak followed by apple crumble from her mum's recipe. It would be the last time Liam would have visitors when on his own. Liam thought later that it was the night that Mark and Fiona looked cosy, like a couple. And Roxy made a play for Jamie which was nothing new. As Mark said to Liam 'we await development.'

It was Jamie who suggested Amsterdam for Liam's stag.

'All that wacky baccy and wanton women.'

When Mark said he was up for it, the decision was made. Petra, surprisingly, wasn't pushed; boys will be boys!

'You may as well have one last fling before I get my hands on you.' she smiled.

'Is that a threat or a promise?

'Both.'

'Besides, Fiona is organising my hen for Saturday, so look out London.'

They were having tea at the Ritz followed by dinner in the West End. Then it was off to the theatre to see Les Misérables. The rest was a secret even she didn't know; it turned out to be Ronnie Scott's and all that jazz!

Jamie had booked the flights for the Friday; to get acclimatised his excuse. He managed to find a seedy hotel in the suburbs of Red-Light land. They opted for the hotel bar that night, pacing themselves as for a race. They had their usual quota of three pints, Amstel for Amsterdam, before turning in. Liam rang Petra from the reception phone to check in and wish her a good hen.

Next morning after a meagre meal they hired out bicycles to ride the canals. Jamie was singing 'Tulips' cycling one handed into the wind.

After a quick shower they looked for a cafe for lunch; Cafe Cannabis by the sweet smoke that greeted them on entering. Mark had to be talked into staying, worried about his athletic lungs. Jamie reassured him that it wasn't like breathing in the fog of fags. They settled for cannabis infused coffee and a round of suspect sandwiches. The afternoon dragged; it was a waiting game for the stag.

They would start with dinner to soak up any excesses. It took a long lingering look before they found a restaurant. The menus in the windows were all double Dutch to them until they found an Italian.

'My kind of language,' Liam the bi-lingual said.

'With more carbo loading for the stag race,' Mark was in his element.

Pasta, pizza and Soave wine to pass a couple of hours.

Jamie had to be humoured with a visit to the Red-Light district, a rite of passage for a groom. More a riot of punters ogling the ware in the windows. Their scanties illuminated by amber lights. Like the tilly lamp Liam's Grandmother had before the arrival of electricity to her farm.

Mark was saying 'I've never seen anything like it,' his eyes out on stilts.

'Innocents abroad,' Jamie wasn't including himself.

Glad to drag Jamie away they tried a few 'pubs'; not exactly the White Horse. More like cafes full of other stags and hens.

The Red Rose cafe sounded promising with music escaping into the night. A guitarist was playing to an indifferent audience.

'The Dutchman':

'The Dutchman's not the kind of man

To keep his thumb jammed in the dam

That holds his dreams in...

When Amsterdam is golden in the morning...

He thinks the tulips bloom beneath the snow...

Let us go to the banks of the ocean

Where the walls rise above the Zuider Zee.

Long ago I used to be a young man...

The words were like a lyric of loss. Was it about living by a fading memory Liam wondered? The hum of the cafe hindered the words; only the remnants of the song remained. An unfinished symphony, a half-forgotten dream. Was memory the means by which you keep love alive? Sarah surfacing again.

On the way out, Liam dropped a few notes on the edge of the stage. The guitarist smiled his thanks and the stag night ended.

Liam thought he'd got away lightly with not even a headache to nurse in the morning. They only had time for a continental breakfast and a stroll along one canal. Back through the R district as Jamie took to calling it. Not a light to be seen from the naked night before; from the surreal to the sedate.

By noon they had packed their holdalls and were on their way to Schiphol airport.

It was a nervous last month; choosing the music, booking the disco for the reception, drawing up the list of people to invite. Only a handful from Ireland, Liam thought. All my friends are here now; it was as if exile had estranged him. They chose the Civil Service club for the reception, a short drive from town. One of the middle-distance squad did the disco, He called himself 'The Sultan of Sing' As Jamie remarked 'better than Derek the Dust' but not by much according to Mark. Petra booked a double room at the Airport hotel for their first night. They would be flying out to a honeymoon in Jersey in the morning. Liam made a trip to London for his wedding suit and called on Aunt Una to ask could Angie be a flower girl at the wedding. She was squealing and literally ran into his arms for her 'big hug'.

The day finally arrived with butterflies in Liam's stomach. It was a bit like lining up for a 1500m, but this was longer, the race of life. He was restless when he awoke for the last time alone. He knew there was only one thing for it. He pulled on his shorts and a tee-shirt with a motif of Che Guevarra that Jamie gave him. It was as if he was dressed for war instead of his wedding day. He jogged down the Boulevard past the golf course and on to the Esplanade. The briny breeze cleared his head and he reversed course at the Pier and picked up the pace on the return. He was in the shower when Mark rang to confirm the time he would be around to drive to the church. He could barely stomach a breakfast and just had a strong coffee instead. As soon as he had put on his wedding suit and knotted his tie several times it was time. The last thought in his mind as he left with Mark was Sarah. He had tried desperately all morning not to think of her, but she came unbidden all the same.

When Petra entered the church, she was wearing a flowing white dress. On her head was a small white hat that looked like a skull cap, perched on the crown of her head. Liam was transported back to Israel, to Sarah's side. He had to gather himself for the ceremony but couldn't take his eyes off Petra's head. He never, ever asked what the hat symbolised, if anything. It was just uncanny on this day of all days. Did he read too much into a hat that matched her dress? Imagining an image of Israel, a symbol of Sarah.

Mark did the honours as the best man and Fiona was the bridesmaid. Although Angie upstaged them both as the flower girl. She insisted on sticking close to Petra and took her hand as they paraded down the aisle. The photographer insisted that Jamie stand at the back for the group photo. Liam asked Mark what was that all about as Jamie had kept a low profile up to then. Mark replied that he didn't have a 'scoobie doo'.

It wasn't until Jamie came up to offer his congratulations that the shabby penny dropped. Petra took a double take before recovering as Jamie planted a kiss on her cheek. Liam and Mark exchanged looks of utter disbelief. Jamie had turned up for the wedding dressed well below the nines. He was resplendent in baggy jeans and a 'Free Nelson Mandela' tee-shirt. Mark elbowed Liam and whispered when he spotted the vision from Vogue.

'You would think that he might put aside his many causes for one day.'

They were in no way surprised, but Jamie did attract a good few stares from the better dressed. Which was everybody but the photographer.

The reception was held in the Civil Service club a short drive from town. Despite his athleticism Liam had two left feet and dreaded the first dance. He was shuffling around telling Petra could only dance in a straight line.

The Sultan played 'Lady in Red' to start the disco.

'But you're wearing white,' Liam whispered in her ear.

'But my undercover is red,' she blushed.

'Oh, right,' he went red as well.

At the end of the night, they left for the Airport Hotel. Tin cans were rattling the road as they drove out of the car park.

When they arrived in Jersey, they caught a taxi to Brelade Bay. The hotel was perched precariously on a cliff top. When Petra went for a shower Liam went back downstairs to check the dining room. He could hear loud cheering coming from the lounge.

The All-Ireland. He'd forgotten it was on Kerry versus Tyrone. South and North or war by other means. The loudness came from a group of men. He recognised the harsh Ulster accents. He sat well away from them, quietly even when Kerry scored. The lounge went quiet as well, as Kerry ran away with another All-Ireland. Liam went out as quietly as he came in thinking there were two occasions to celebrate tonight.

They spent the week exploring the island; it didn't take long to circle it in the hired car. They took a boat trip to Sark, a trip into the past. Pastoral. No cars allowed so they took a tour in a horse drawn carriage. On the way back, they stopped at a pottery studio where Petra bought a bowl and a lamp. Liam was reminded of the tilly lamp his grandmother had on her dresser.

On their last day Petra wanted to see Grosnez Castle; she called it 'the big nose'. Lastly, La Corbiere lighthouse which they remembered; backing Corbiere to win the Grand National. On the way back, they came across a camera crew filming an episode of Bergerac. Petra thought she recognised the lead actor, but Liam had never seen it, so didn't know him. 'Sorry,' he said but Petra just smiled 'for what?'

Liam was concerned that Petra wouldn't settle into the confines of a flat, but she wasn't one bit phased and soon re-arranged the bachelor pad. It was only a matter of changing the furniture to make the rooms look bigger.

For the first year of married life the training slackened off. With Petra's close to Cordon Bleu cooking Liam put on a few pounds, losing the gaunt look. In Jamie's words he was barely ticking over, just four runs a week.

'But I am running a department,' he retorted smugly to Jamie.

'Now behave, children,' Mark said as Jamie made a meow sound.

Liam wondered was it always the case, but the first year flew. First holiday together in Rome; the pasta, the piazza and the vino. The Trevi Fountain, the Spanish Steps and the Colosseum. Petra wanted to see the Vatican and the hotel booked the Pope's general audience on Wednesday. The crowds surged forward when he careered around the square in his popemobile. It was just as if a rock star was performing as they were shunted forward like a rugby maul.

They both thought it was in Rome that their son was conceived. Petra put it down to the Italian warmth and wine. Later Liam was convinced when the little Luigi showed an aptitude for football. When Petra found out for certain it was going to be a boy, they wrote down a list of names. James, John, Cian and Killian. Liam slipped in Mario at the end of the list and Petra couldn't believe her eyes.

'You're joking, surely you can't be serious?'

'Well, the reason being he must have started his voyage in Italy.'

'So, why not Sinbad then?' she had him.

In the end they decided on 'Conor'. They were still mulling the names over when 'Tears in Heaven' was playing on the radio. The DJ said it was about Eric Clapton's son who fell from a balcony in New York, Conor. It was decided by the time the last plaintive notes had faded.

When Petra was off on maternity leave, they decided to sell the flat. It took months to sell as the market was sluggish. Eventually they were able to do their own viewing after agreeing a reduced price for the flat. Most weekends were taken up with looking through three-bedroom houses. Discussing the plus and minus of each viewing. After a couple of months, they found a bungalow overlooking Priory Park. Looking out from the small patio the park was so close that it looked like an extension of the garden. Perfect for Petra who struggled with stairs. Liam had already mapped out a fartlek route round the perimeter of the park. The box room was converted into a nursery for the arrival of Conor and the spare room into a study for Liam. He had no excuse for not continuing with his writing now. Perhaps he could move up from the short story to the novel. The athletic analogy of middle to long distance running. Once settled he upped his training to be able to stay with Mark and Jamie.

Shortly after they moved to Priory Park a re-directed letter with 'Please Do Not Bend' on it arrived. Liam was glad it was Saturday as Petra was in town shopping with her sister. A photo fell out when he opened the buff envelope. A young woman in an army uniform smiling back at him. She was holding an M16 rifle across her chest. He scarcely recognised Inbar from the feisty young girl he remembered.

Sarah had included a note to let him know that Inbar now knew he was her father. When Sarah had sat her down before she commenced her military training, she had sensed something.

'Leem is my dad?

'Sababa, cool,' she had hugged Sarah.

She had sensed there was more than friendship between them. Were they not hugging that last night in Mishmar? Sarah went on to say that Inbar had taken it all in her stride.

'Must be taking after you if you pardon the pun,' she added.

Then when Sarah produced the pendant Inbar kissed it ' for luck' before Sarah fastened it behind her neck. Inbar was wearing his emerald pendant underneath her uniform now. Sarah went on to say that Inbar sends her love and mine too as always. Her p.s was to congratulate him on his marriage.

Shortly before Conor was born another letter with an Israeli postmark arrived. This time Petra picked it up and she told him it was from a friend who stayed behind after he left the kibbutz. He consoled himself that the white lie was true to a certain extent. He waited until Petra was out the door with her sister for her last scan at the hospital.

On opening the letter his eyes swept over the words: Inbar...Intifada... Injured? Her patrol had come under attack in the West Bank, on the outskirts of Nablus. A sixteen-year-old Palestinian boy hurled a random rock directly at her chest. After dragging her away her Captain opened the top of her uniform. The pendant fell to the ground, shattered like tiny diamonds in the dust. The medics told Sarah that the pendant had saved her life. In the end she was invalidated out of the army. After recovering in Mishmar Ha Sharon she left for Jerusalem to train to be a nurse.

'So, I'm back on my own again,' Sarah finished the letter. Was it a hint?

Liam wrote back straight away with a 'get well' card for Inbar. He included another 100-dollar money order 'to replace the pendant'. At the same time, he told her that very soon he would have a son.

'If you wish you may tell Inbar that she will have a half-brother.'

As he finished the letter he doubted if he could tell Conor about his sister in Israel. If only half. As for Petra? He knew it would be impossible to divulge his secret. Before posting the letter, he put their new address on the back. To keep in touch just in case Sarah wanted to. And his daughter, his Inbar.

They were barely settled in their new house when Sarah answered his letter. A thank you note to tell him that she bought Inbar another pendant. How well she was doing in

Jerusalem with a new boyfriend, a Palestinian trainee doctor. Congratulating him on the birth of his son but perhaps keeping it from Inbar.

Finally, that Gene was moving from HaOgen to Mishmar as a fully-fledged kibbutznik. Sarah had taught him the basics of Hebrew and he had moved in with her. No mention of marriage Liam thought as he finished reading what would be her last letter. So, they were both with strangers now.

Outside of a few sleep disturbed nights Conor was a dream baby. Petra took to motherhood as if she were born for it. Liam had a surge of feeling when he first held the little bundle for the first time. His little face scrunched up as he looked at Liam; he's wondering who you are was Petra's take. Liam was regretting not being there when Inbar was born away in Israel, as he held his son.

In his early years Conor was like a lapdog after Liam. His constant companion; me and my shadow as Petra would say as they came back from the park. Liam would take him on the short walk around the road to the park when he was doing intervals. Even at four his short little legs would try to keep up. Liam would let him run while he walked the recoveries.

Connor wanted to be a runner like Mark. He had figured that Mark was the better of the other two when he saw them running together on a Sunday morning. Then he wanted to be a footballer when he started school and was kicking a ball in the playground. After that it was a postman and a policeman because of the uniforms. But when Jamie turned up in his fireman's gear it was definitely a fireman!

Then when he was in junior school, he joined a Sunday morning team. Togged out in proper football shirt and shorts he looked slight but nippy. He would fly along the wing and put over crosses like Beckham. All the tall gangly centre forward had to do was guide the flight to the net. When Liam managed to attend a match after a long run and saw Conor haring down the wing he knew why. Intervals he attributed his speed endurance to when the rest of his team were puffed out.

On Sunday afternoons they would sit together on the settee to watch a game on TV. Petra would be laughing at how serious they would take the result. Liam would say it was a mystery only men could understand.

Then, 'Conor would you explain the offside rule to your mother again?'

When Man U were playing the Hammers, they were ribbing each other as rivals. Liam being a Manchester United fan since Munich. Conor was a West Ham fan simply to fit in with his mates whose parents weren't long out of the East End.

It must have been when Conor was sixteen when he changed from being an obliging boy to a sullen son. Teenage troubles as Petra was inclined to put it or existential angst Sarah would say. Liam thought he was just being a rebel without a cause. A bit like Jamie in a way who had multiple issues to champion. So, there was no more running with Liam, no more football matches on Sunday mornings. His schoolwork was also on a downward trajectory. Liam told him he'd be like Dell boy's brother with his two GCE's. If he didn't buck up his ideas, he'd be down the local market trying to turn another buck.

He started going out to disco's and returning late with a whiff of alcohol seeping from his bedroom. Even when Petra grounded him for a couple of weekends it made no odds. Then when Liam smelled the smoky sweet smell of cannabis, they knew it was a problem. Petra read him the riot act to no avail. Liam regretted taking a backseat even though he knew Conor would pan him off with another excuse. It was only a matter of time and they were just waiting for the inevitable.

Every time Conor went out, they were waiting for the phone call or worse the knock on the door.

It was on Petra's birthday in late September that the doorbell rang. Conor had presented her with a bouquet of roses and a necklace with a butterfly motif. Liam had bought her earrings to match. The three of them were laughing at the coincidence although Petra had thought they had colluded. Just two men without imagination Liam told her winking at Conor. Then the doorbell rang to disturb their intimate unity.

Later Liam would think of Hemingway's 'For Whom The Bell Tolls'. For it tolled for Conor that evening. The evening that changed everything, that changed their lives forever.

Liam answered while Conor was pouring a glass of bubbly for Petra. A former teammate of Conor's, the centre forward, stood there. He was fidgeting on his feet as if waiting for Conor to cross the ball. His hair had grown long and lank. His averted eyes were swivelling in his head.

'Is Con in?' he muttered Conor's diminutive. All their surnames ending like George being Besty.

'Stanley, I didn't recognise you for a second there,' Liam was staring.

'How's the form, any goals lately?' Liam continued.

'Good, no goals now.' Stanley looked to the ground as if to find the ball.

'I ain't playing football anymore,' he sounded regretful.

'That's a shame Stan, you were lethal in your time.'

'I'll get Conor for you,' Liam turned back inside.

'Cheers Lim,' getting the name wrong, not for the first time.

Liam was reminded of Inbar and her 'Leem'. But at least Stan smiled for the first time like he did when he nodded to the net. When Conor came to the door, they high fived each other another football field ritual they shared. Liam couldn't hear as they had a whispered conflab.

Liam noticed that Conor only directed his request to Petra.

'Mum, Stan wants me to go to a party in town with him,' he pleaded. 'A mate's twenty first,' he added for effect.

'Off you go then and Conor, behave,' she waved him off.

'And not too late back,' she called after him.

'I shan't be, thanks Mum.'

'I better change then, must look the part,' he bounded upstairs.

He came down wearing blue jeans, a black tee shirt and white Nikes.

'You didn't overdo it then,' Petra smiled as he came into the lounge.

'Smart but casual as the cliche goes,' he kissed her cheek.

On the way out he high fived Liam who scuffed his gelled hair.

'If you can't be good, be careful,' Liam called after him.

'Bye, bye,' and he was gone.

They waited up until Match of the Day, United scraped a draw at Anfield. Banter with Roxy on Monday? Petra finally gave up saying he can return in his own good time. Liam read another chapter of 'Where the Jackals Howl'; it was taking an age to get through it. Neither of them heard him come in; he probably closed the door quietly for a change. They could imagine him creeping in and crashing out, fully dressed as usual.

Liam was up at eight for a quick sluice and a strong coffee before Mark and Jamie came knocking. The sky was riddled with rain; soft summer drops measured out the morning. After five miles patches of blue covered the clouds and the sun suddenly broke free. Jamie upped the tempo for the second section. He had read that was how the Kenyan's trained on their long runs.

'What's good enough for the gazelles of Africa is better for us,' Jamie sprinted ahead.

'Jamie is doing a tempo temporus,' Liam was apt to break into pidgin Latin.

'You 're killing me with that dead language,' Mark would be shaking his head.

'As for Haile Gebrselassie ahead, highly unlikely he'll still be in front at the end.'

The words were hardly out of his mouth when Jamie blew up and sheepishly fell back to the steady pace.

When they all diverged at the park Liam jogged the last few yards home, a pleasant heaviness in his legs. On exiting the park, he noticed a squad car parked near the gate. Yobbus Britannicus or the winos? He was thinking it was a bit unusual to see the police out on a Sunday in their 'jam jar'. As he came around the corner by the roundabout, he saw Petra standing at the door. He was going to say "what's up nosey parker" to her for a laugh. There was someone on the far side of her and when he came closer saw that it was a policewoman.

'Conor,' his heart jolted in his chest, starting up again after his run.

'What's the matter?' he called from a distance.

Petra held back until he opened the gate and half stumbled towards him.

'It's Conor.' her eyes were red.

It looked like there was blood seeping from them, highlighting the brown. The policeman drove the squad to park outside the house. He shook hands with Liam ' Sorry sir.'

'Shall we go inside?' the young policewoman said.

They were mindful of the stares coming from the cars on the roundabout, mercifully few.

'Bloody rubbernecks, pardon my French,' the policeman banged the door behind him.

When they were all seated in the lounge it was the policeman who spoke, very slowly. In the early hours, an ambulance had been called to a house in the middle of town. Liam knew it as the Red Centre but nothing like Australia. A young man had been discovered in the bathroom. He was sprawled and unresponsive to the medics.

'Is he?' Liam hesitated, fearing the answer.

'We don't know yet sir,' the policeman said gently.

'If you wish we can drive you to the A&E'?

Liam hurriedly pulled on a pair of tracksters and a hooded top while Petra went as she was. He hadn't realised that he was getting cold, the sweat drying into the small of his back. On the way the policeman asked them did they know Stanley Jones. Petra answered first from the back seat where she was sitting with the policewoman.

'Yes, he used to be best mates with Conor from playing football together.'

Liam added that Stan had called the previous evening to invite Conor to a house party.

'Did either of you know that Mr. Jones is a dealer in hard drugs?'

They were so shocked to hear this that they couldn't answer for a moment.

'No, not at all,' they were talking over each other.

'Was actually, not 'is' now,' the policeman clarified.

'Mr. Jones was arrested last night in the house your son was found in.'

'He was dealing at the party supplying a Class A drug.'

'Bit of form, has our Stanley,' The policeman said drily.

That would explain the hollow eyes and shifty demeanour Liam thought.

'To reassure you, there is no evidence your son, Conor is it? was involved.'

'He was just the latest victim of the scourge of drugs, especially the hard variety,' the policeman finished.

The squad stopped outside the A&E and the policewoman went in first. She beckoned them in when she emerged. Liam was trying to read her face, but it was impassive, in repose.

'Would you be alright to get a taxi back home?' the policeman was opening Petra's door.

'Yes, that's fine by us; thanks so far,' Liam eased his stiff legs out.

The policewoman patted Petra's arm as they passed and headed for the entrance.

'Mind how you go,' the policeman waved and was away.

A severe faced woman was looking up as they approached the reception.

'Mrs and Mr Lucid?'

They both answered 'yes,' and she turned to a uniformed man standing by the desk.

'Please come with me,' he said by way of explanation.

They followed him down a long corridor, both silent. On opening a door at the end, they found themselves outside again.

They were led towards a flat roofed building separate from the Main. A severe aspect to it suggested only one thing to Liam: the morgue. He caught hold of Petra's hand, tightly, as if he didn't want her to enter. The uniformed man, ambulance service, was it? held the door open for them. He quickly walked to what looked like a table with a white cloth across it. A shroud? That's how they eventually found their only son. Laid out on a slab not a table. Not a tablecloth, a shroud. Petra uttered a small searing sound. Hardly human in the silence. Liam felt cold and numb, felt nothing. The ambulance man pulled back the shroud, slowly, slowly to reveal the reality.

Conor looked so young, almost like a child again. A faint flush to his cheeks. Looking for all the world as if he had just fallen asleep. Forever. Petra leaned over to touch his hair. To leave a soft kiss on his cold cheek. Leaving a teardrop to fall as if he was weeping. Liam could only touch his forehead under his floppy fringe. They turned, looking at each other, like strangers, for the first time. When Petra broke down, they were shaking and shuddering against each other. Life as they knew it when they arose that morning had ended for them too. It was anti nature to bury your child as they knew they must.

The ambulance man looked embarrassed at the emotion, looking away from them. Silently they were led back to the woman at the desk.

She said she was sorry but there was a process to go through.

'A process' how cold, how clinical, they were both thinking, but unsaid. A sudden death inquest after an autopsy which could take weeks. It would be well into Autumn, the season when the year began to decay.

'The body should be released by the middle of October.'

'That's the best estimate I can offer, 'she was very business-like.

No 'sorry for your trouble.' Liam made a decision there and then to take Conor home. To rest with his grandfather, whom he was very fond of. In the early years Conor would follow his Grandad around the farm on the long summer holidays. Watching the old man milk the cows the old-fashioned way. Up to then Conor had thought that milk came from the Co-Op. Liam wondered how best to approach the subject with Petra. She might want Conor's grave to be near, to lay flowers on his birthday and such.

In the end she agreed with his plan as she blamed his friends, especially Stan. She didn't want them anywhere near for his funeral. She would only allow the school to organise a guard of honour when the time came for his final journey.

Liam went sick on the Monday after phoning in pre-empting anyone finding out in the local newspaper. The Chief Executive Officer told him to take as much time as he needed for what was necessary. He'd make sure his time off would come under compassionate and not sick leave. When he did return to work people didn't know what to say; he only endured their stares. Only Fiona and Roxy came up to his desk to sympathise. Fiona shook his hand, but Roxy gave him a hug in full view of the office.

Mark and Jamie came around to visit and sat with them for an hour. They both embraced Petra and shook Liam's hand and patted him on the shoulder when they left. They both had great time for Conor and spoke of his early ambition of being a runner and then a fireman, taking after Mark and Jamie.

A reporter from the local paper called looking for a story. 'A comment will do,' as he said. Petra called it insensitive in the extreme and Liam, politely, showed him the door. In any event it was splattered all over the next edition which implied that Conor was selling drugs with his mate. That he was Stan's wingman in the enterprise. The irony of the word wingman wasn't lost on Liam. But Stan was scoring more than goals now.

Conor's last adventure was described as 'misadventure' by the coroner. They had to listen to official and officious way it was worded. The autopsy had already revealed that Conor had injected, probably for the first time given the reaction. So, he had progressed from smoking pot to the hard drug of heroin.

Afterwards, Liam wanted to bring him back to the bungalow, even for one night. He had the traditional wake in mind until Petra pointed out that there was no such ritual around here. In the end they went back to the morgue to say a final goodbye and close the coffin. At least nobody would be gawking at him Liam consoled himself. When the lid was lowered Petra leaned her head on it and kissed the front where his head would be. Liam just patted the gleaming oak and gently helped Petra up.

The arrangements were complex, Essex to London for the flight, then Dublin to Kerry by hearse. Aer Lingus was the only airline that took remains. Conor would travel on his own; they had booked a flight for next day. The last lap for Conor; they would be with him to the finishing line.

Liam and Petra were invited to a memorial service in the assembly hall at Conor's school. It was Mr Abdul as he was nicknamed who called around to ask them. He was Conor's favourite teacher mainly as he would let him off early for football training. He asked them to suggest any music they would like for Conor. Liam chose the origin of Conor's name, the lost name he was called after. 'Tears in Heaven'. Petra had been to see Les Misérables in the West End and loved 'Bring him Home'.

It was a mainly secular service with a chaplain reciting the 'Our Father' at the end.

They left with the tenor voice of the choir searing the words from Les Misérables in their ears.

Bring him peace, bring him joy

He is young, he is only a boy

You can take, you can give

Let him be, let him live.

Bring him home,

Bring him home.

The school lined up outside the hospital as the hearse drove slowly out the gate. A guard of honour led by the captain of the school football team. They started clapping as if Conor had scored a winning goal.

Dublin skyline sketched blue in the last remnants of the day. The October evening stretched towards night. The wet wind from the Liffey freshened as it swept along O'Connell Street. Dust and voices lifted in its wake. Crowds were still swarming around bus stops. The last of the season's backpackers heading for the Airport. Going south like migrating birds seeking the sun.

Liam had an idea that there were B&B's on the way to Bus Aras. Their cases made them feel self-conscious. They had been warned about Dublin. It wasn't always the friendly town of the tourist board. Twenty years or so nobody was talking about drugs. The only mugger was the Minister who raised taxes in the budget. Sometimes, miraculously from the dead.

The ritual rites of the funeral surfaced. Liam had stared at the morning moist fields as they floated past the train. The summer green still lingering on the land, clinging to life. Leaving behind the white- washed oak in the brown earth. 'Tears in Heaven' playing again; a requiem. A second requiem of rain falling like tears on earth. The pious prayers; the riddle of the rosary. What did it mean in the heel of the hunt?

The train from Killarney shunting them away after the funeral lunch. The Kingdom Hotel bar loud with the sound of American voices.

A grub faced paperboy stood at the traffic lights, chanting.

'Press, Herald, all the 'newds,' mister.'

When Petra stopped to change hands, the boy thrust a paper at Liam, like a sword. He bought a Herald but couldn't understand the boy's lisping language when he asked for directions.

Seventeen quid the miser charged. Must think we're bloody tourists, Petra's accent. Liam wondered was there a plural for 'punt'. Seventeen punts; it didn't sound right. Right robbery more like Liam thought.

Petra was shattered from the emotion of the day, eyes red raw, her heart aching in agony. She wouldn't be hungry for dinner, having had a stale roll on the train. The trolly dolly made them smile for the first time that day.

You fo'coffee?' she said to Petra.

Was she swearing they were asking each other when the trolley passed on?

Petra wouldn't be persuaded to go out again but if Liam could get a bag of chips that would do. He could see that that was only one hunger in her heart. She had lost part of herself; it was she who had carried Conor into the world. They had both lost their sense of each other. They wouldn't be able to repair themselves in the future. As someone once wrote ' the past is a foreign country'. They would be foreigners to each other in a strange land. Racked with the guilt of losing their only child. And Liam, alone, to heal his other, hidden hurt.

By the time Liam had freshened up it was getting on for seven. Ready to stroll up Grafton Street, have a meal, maybe a jar. They would spend another day in Dublin before facing the deadly dullness over. No hurry back to the languor of London, the eejits of Essex. Liam was already correcting himself for his intolerant thoughts as they surfaced in his mind.

He had forgotten what it was like to be out on a Saturday night. He'd read that Dublin was a young city. Grafton Street was giddy with girls. In a side street he slipped in for a pint. The bar was bulging with bonhomie. At a few years shy of fifty he felt almost young. He thought he could nearly be his son.

He wandered back towards O'Connell Street. A busker was playing 'Raglan Road' outside Bewley's. His father used to sing that song:

'And I said, let grief be a fallen leaf at the dawning of the day."

At a random restaurant, he found a table for two inside the window. He ordered a steak and a carafe of white wine. He

213

watched a gang of youths keeping company with the floozie in the jacuzzi. He thought my son could be amongst them, in their anonymous uniforms. In sweatshirts, jeans and trainers. Instead...

His steak arrived sizzling; the waitress smiled, and he was won. It must be the way she tossed her fair fringe that reminded him of Sarah. Or was that Marion; it must have been the day that was in it. Marion? She'd be forty this Christmas. Life beginning... What a bloody ironic cliche. Taken by the tropic of cancer. He thought he might buy a ticket later. Life being a lottery you never know.

Wine warmed like a summer memory. 'In vino veritas'. There was something tangible about today. A generic gap he couldn't bridge. Was it the thought of Marion, Conor? His son in the end game of life. The wine reflected his father's pallid pain as he shook hands in farewell.

'Good luck Liam, write to your mother.'

Flower Power flourished in the Summer of Love. The year the six-day war raged over Sarah and the daughter he didn't know he had. He wore green grandad vests with white cords. His sun-bleached hair tumbled over his freckled forehead. At Civil Service parties' joints and joss sticks mingled. Poems appeared in the International Times. The tanned thighs of girls provoked on double decker buses. At Grosvenor Square blood flowed for Vietnam. When he first saw Marion there was a river of red flowing through her hair. A horse's hoof had glanced off her head as she fell in the melee. She grabbed Liam's hand and they scrambled away. He waited while she was bandaged in St.

Barth's. When they met again there was music and flowers in Hyde Park.

There was a soft edge to her accent, from Clare. She worked in Willesden Green library, book stacking as she said. If there was a demonstration Liam would travel up from Essex on Friday night and return on late on Sunday. They started to go to concerts, sometimes with her friend Mona. Thin Lizzy at the Rainbow. The Stones at Hyde Park. Saturday nights in Co. Kilburn. Sunday strolls besides the turgid Thames. The wound of Vietnam would heal; they left the demo days behind.

In retrospect they were the most platonic of pals. Never holding hands and only a chaste peck on the cheek on parting. Were they both wondering about each other?

In the summer they went on holiday together in Clare and Kerry, resurrecting their roots. Aer Lingus was delayed at Heathrow, just made the train in Cork. They ran into rain in Killarney sweeping over the huddle of hills. The road twisting and turning; the sea expanding to Dingle. French students cramming the bus; singing 'Je Ne Regrette Rien', as a sheer drop appeared on a bend. The girls thrusting their breasts out in front of farmers. Liam heard one old man mutter 'brazen hoors' as he got off.

The sun was searching the hills as they got off at Caragh Bridge. The river dancing in an evening breeze. The hay was saved in the Upper Meadow, the wynds in even rows. A reek of turf cast a shadow at the gable end of the farmhouse. Passing the hawthorn bush at the gate they entered another world. Liam's mother was in the kitchen fussing over her hair. His father in the Furze Field at the back of the haggard. His sister,

Aine, would be home for her holidays, her girlhood gone. White wine and Sweet Afton; sheer nylons and Channel. She wafted through the world in purple and perfume.

Beer and ballads in lounge bars. James Connolly and James Taylor: fire and rain. Bleeding history for silver. Soccer in the summer evenings. Noticing changes as brilliant bungalows glowed from once green fields. Tame flowers growing neatly along straight borders. Television aerials tangling with turf smoke. People conversing with flickering images. The North would get nearer; Down had already won another All-Ireland.

A new decade dawned. Spring was slowly stretching the days when the message was left on his desk.

'Father accident, contact sister.'

When Liam rushed back to the flat a telegram lay on the mat.

'Dad dead, please come home.'

He couldn't think. Aine, Aer Lingus, Marion? He had the phone in his hand for an age; started to dial, stopped. When he eventually rang Aine, a man answered. He left a message and rang Marion. Straight away she said she'd book two seats on the first Aer Lingus flight. He poured a nip of brandy left over from Christmas. He had a strange image of his father in the Upper Field. Still. While waiting for Marion to get back he went to the local barber. His hair was laying like hay across his shoulders. Shorn like a sheep he heard the phone ringing as he entered the flat. He had four hours to get to Heathrow, Marion would be there with the flight tickets.

His mother's face like yellow ashes in a black range. Aine, a thin pinched look behind a mourning veil. Repeating over and over again the details of the day. How he went down to the River Field. It was the Friesian that had to be fettered for milking that caused him to lose his footing.

'He was at the height of his glory,' his mother kept repeating. They had planned to go to town that evening. He was due for Confession while she gathered the messages. Afterwards, they would have a drink and a singsong in the Corner house.

A hackney was hired to drive them to the mortuary later. After a moment looking at the coffin, they went to the Kingdom Hotel. Hands hurried towards them as they entered one by one.

'Sorry for your trouble.'

The shock surfacing suddenly as Liam shook hands with the farmer next door. Tears at his eyelids; only Marion noticed. When he ordered the drinks, brandy bled in his veins.

A hardy March morning. The daffodils danced in ditches. Aine frying reams of rashers. Relatives arriving; farmer's fidgeting with their caps in the kitchen. Shouldering him over the bridge. Soaking in a sun shower. Crossing the river; the Rubicon. A rapid rosary rang out. A ridge of earth waiting. Clods clumping on the oak. His mother lost on a tide of tears.

Afterwards, attending a lunch at the hotel; ham and eggs, soda bread, tea and talk. Etching his memory with anecdote. Picking up the fragments; filling in the wounds.

War over London. Arrogated into the British army. Deserting in Devon. Hunted home. Defended by Dev. Coming into land on the death of his father. Finding a country girl at a crossroads dance. Shy, slender, with chestnut hair brightened by the sun.

Ascetic years, harvesting hope. Husbanding the meagre land. The twins born in the upper room. Whooping cough claiming them inside six months. Burying two little bodies in a week. A boy at the beginning and a girl at the end; grieving at the grave for years. Liam and Aine arriving after the fallow years; surrogate souls.

People drifted away; they walked back to the grave to detach the cards from the wreaths. Marion was linking his mother when they got back to the hotel.

The farm was silent; Aine washed up with Marion in the kitchen after a light supper. Liam helped a neighbour's son do the milking. He left the cranky cow to the boy. He moped around while the women went for a lie-down. It was getting on for nine when they surfaced. Liam decided to go to town again, alone.

He borrowed his father's bike from the turf shed. The Raleigh was rusty; the dynamo missed the rim of the back wheel. Rain reached across the river as he freewheeled down to the bridge. He imagined the cold water seeping through the mound. He shivered and the bike swerved towards the river.

Beer and brandy after hours. Holding the numb night at bay. The moon throwing menacing shadows from the ditches as he wheeled the bike home. By Caragh bridge he stopped, watching the water wending to the sea. The silence interrupted by the splash of waves over stones. Did he smell woodbine, Spring germinating? Blue bells and buttercups. Fox's fingers pointing in ditches. The ephemeral feel of bog cotton. The fullness and fragility of life. Tears tumbled into the dark river.

In his summer leave he came home for the hay. Marion headed for the Burren tracing her ancestors. Aine got engaged to a bank manager. Changes. Liam spent long days in the meadows. Sweat and sweet tea. Bringing back his boyhood. Jumping on the wynds for joy, for his father. Loving him without words in the evening when he was allowed to take the reins. The horse impatient for the road, snorting and shaking the harness.

Dazzling days in Whitestrand when the hay was saved. Running ten laps, over and back to keep in touch with his fading fitness. Sometimes joined by the local legend who would run for Ireland.

Watching the regatta off the pier. The Seine boats cutting the water like returning Vikings. Three card tricks and three horse races in the Island course. Nijinsky had already etched his image over Epsom, dancing away with the Derby.

'Jesus Nijinsky!' There was a memory. The equine icon. When was it? The first of June 1970. To be remembered ... Like he remembered his father in a field. Was this the male menopause he wondered? Time slipping away in the All-Ireland.

He poured the last drops of the carafe. It's strange the events you remember. In no chronological order. Just the random musings of memory. Like listening to Sports Stadium on Radio Eireann when Kennedy was shot in '63. Watching 'Gandhi' with his mother. The movie interrupted by Bloody

Sunday. The priest waving a bloody hankie. Thirteen dead; then fourteen. History.

The wine made him feel light-headed. The wide expanse of O'Connell Street condensed. He felt homesick like when he first emigrated to Essex. He was trying to make connections. Caught between his father and his son. He drained the wine. It felt like dredging the river.

Looking for answers. A boy of sixteen, pock-marked with pain. No solution to life at the bottom of a glass. His father used to say that, and he could sink a fair few pints in his day. Both ending up at the bottom whether by accident or designer drug.

Liam looked out to O'Connell Street twirling the stem of the empty wine glass. He could see the water from the fountain bubbling around the cold body of Anna Livia. He saw his father again in the River Field. Afraid of water; never swam. He imagined his son diving in to save him. That's what memory was for, to deal a different hand, to trump reality. He'd buried them both; he would remember in unquiet moments.

Like Nijinsky on a Wednesday, Kennedy on a Friday, Gandhi on a Sunday. History repeated.

He paid the rip-off bill; the place was still crowded. He felt stiff from sitting, suddenly old in this young city. The spray from the fountain splattered his face as he crossed O'Connell Street. Anonymous and ancient: who would remember him? More than anything he wanted to be identified. To be given a name for eternity. he wanted to be remembered by his son. Like on the avenues of exile when he saw his father in a field. Still...

EPILOGUE
'regret belong to the past'

The flood of memories carried Liam around the city. Stopping at South Terrace with its silent synagogue.

'Chocolate-coloured paint and the July sun
like a blowtorch peeling off
the last efforts of love.
More than time has abandoned this.
To sit here now in the rancid sunshine
of low tide is to interiorise
all of the unnoticed work of love.

Exquisite children fall like jewels
from an exhausted colporteur's bag.
Where these jewels fall beside the peeling door
let us place the six lilies of memory,
the six wounds of David's peeling star.'

He smiled ironically at the notion of meeting Sarah coming from Mass up Summerhill. Instead, she was worshiping here with her parents on the Sabbath. He was a day out and a millennium of miles from her culture.

The Mall, the Grand Parade and back along Panna. Soft summer clouds called over the Lee. A freshening breeze disturbed the water at Patrick's bridge. The still empty Coliseum like a monument to memory. The past being a foreign country; accessed by the bridge ahead. Along McCurtain Street to St. Patrick's Quay. The Mary Elmes bridge to Merchant's Quay.

Was this called after the brave woman who defied the Nazis? The Mary of the Pyrenees who saved Sarah's father from the gas chambers. Down Harley Street Liam walked slowly across the memorial to Mary thinking what if? There would be no Sarah in the world for him; on that cold crossing he gave thanks for Mary Elmes.

Retracing his steps, he ascended Summerhill as he had done so many times as a student. Sarah's house was in darkness; he could just make out the name, the sign faded over the years.

'Mizpah,' her Watchtower.

'May the Lord watch between me and thee when apart from one another.'

Turning at the still, silver railings of St. Luke's church and on to Wellington Road. Ardagh House was in darkness as he forced the key in the lock, rattling open the door. Petra was fast asleep, one hand outstretched as if in supplication. When he saw her dark head against the pillow he was instantly lacerated with longing.

For the brilliant blonde hair fanning out on the grass in the Glen. For the way Sarah turned in his hands, moist lips clinging. Her breasts tumbling from her flimsy blouse, nipples hardening in his hands. The satin softness flattening across his chest. A hand reaching for the tenderness of her opening thighs. Cupping the silken softness as her hips urged upwards. He could feel her body pulsing beneath him. A medley of moans escaping her open lips. He was poised above her, waiting to fill the emptiness.

When he was inside her he rested there for a moment. It was if he wanted to be one with her, to reach her core. Then she arched her hips, and he was thrusting deeper and deeper. He was, momentarily embarrassed to slip out but she quickly reached down to guide him home. He was on the edge then, their futures formed. Poised in a moment of release and regret.

'We were lonely for each other,' she had said in Galilee.

Feeling the void in the night.

Walking towards a restless sunset.

Into an existential evening; dusk to darkness.
To a moment in time.
Time is... so long.

THE END

POSTCRIPT

A good few years after Conor's death and life had wrought many changes. Again. Liam was now on his own in the lonely house; Petra long gone. Try as they might, they couldn't heal each other. The silences getting longer and longer. In the end they had nothing to say to each other. Each with their own private pain; suffering separately. Conor was the gel that held the family together. His absence like a wound that would not heal.

Liam had bought the second share of the house as part of the divorce settlement. The parting was, at least, amicable; they embraced at the door, almost fondly. Petra was moving in with her sister and her husband until she found a little flat. The husband, whom Petra used to call the Fat Controller, was an auctioneer so it wouldn't take long. She went for a property overlooking the Esplanade with a tiny garden.

Soon after the separation Liam took early retirement. The Civil Service was the first target for Tory cuts. He decided to sell up and see his Autumn day's out back home. He would get a collie like Carlo on the farm growing up. A female would be easier; he already had a name for her: Sheba. A queen from what was Sarah's part of the world now. And a Jack Russell for contrast; Rex, the king of small dogs.

Liam still ran for recreation like active mindfulness. Sometimes with Mark for old time's sake, occasionally joined by Jamie. They had to find a new local for the after run jar and the Sunday get together. The White Horse had galloped off in the recession. The Blue Boar or the Red Lion?

'It's like being on safari with you sods,' Jamie joked when they settled on the Lion.

'Now we're living on past glories,' Mark would say wistfully as he raised his glass.

After moving up to the marathon the heavy mileage took its toll on Mark. After running a blinder in London with a sub 2.15 he had a disaster in Chicago and called time on his career.

The bell for his last lap had faded, 'leaving the games of his youth, forever'. He now had time to take up with Fiona. The next bell he heard was plural, wedding bells.

By some strange serendipity Jamie hooked up with Roxy. Miss Ogyny? After all he and Roxy were Marxist/Leninists. So, one Sunday night he quoted Marx on the subject of matrimony.

'Marriage is an institution but who the hell wants to live in an institution?'

His punch line was that it was Groucho not Karl Marx who said it. Liam was wondering how was Roxy a Leninist. She was saying it was because she was a Scouser. But Lenin was a Muscovite Mark was arguing.

'Don't tell me, you mean John Lennon, not whatsit Lenin,' Liam sussed it.

'Vladimir,' Jamie corrected.

'Whatever,' Mark was weary.

Whatever was the ideological reason between Jamie and Roxy, somehow it worked.

After numerous viewings, half the time wasters, Liam accepted a price below the guide price. He knew he would more than make up the difference on the rate of exchange. He arranged a re-direction at the sorting office. He was packing big boxes that the haulage company supplied when the postman knocked early one morning. He thought it must be a recorded delivery, perhaps from the solicitor who did the conveyance.

'Sorry, I wanted to make sure this was yours', the postie held out a crumpled packet.

'It's like your name, Liam innit, but Leem?'

'Sarah', his heart gave a jolt. After all this time. He took the packet, the Israeli stamp but not her handwriting.

'Inbar'?

'Thanks postie, just a spelling mistake in my first name; see Lucid? 'This is for me alright.'

When the postman had gone, he took the packet to the kitchen. He made a cup of coffee and took it into the cluttered lounge. He was savouring the delay in opening it. He finished his coffee before ripping the packet open.

Dear Father,

Sorry for being so formal. I wanted to address you as Papa, but?

I have very sad news to tell you.

Mama had cancer (breast) for the past two years.

She fought hard but in the end her courage wasn't enough.

On last Shabbat she passed away peacefully.

Me and Gene were with her at the end in Netanya hospital.

I was holding her hand when she drew her last breath in this life.

We closed her beautiful eyes together; the gold in them were the last to fade.

I got your address in her locker; she had kept it there all the time.

I think she wanted to write to you, but she was too weak.

Before she passed, she whispered to me to let you know she was going.

She wanted you to know that she loved you from the beginning to the end and into eternity.

We buried her next to Haim in Kfar Haim in Mishmar Ha Sharon.

The Rose of Sharon and a white stone like a Lily covered her coffin as she was laid to rest.

I'm so sorry I have to break this bad news to you, but it was Mama's last wish.

For myself, I'm married and live in Jerusalem. My husband is a Palestinian; he was the young medic who treated me during the last Intifada.

Like Mama and you meeting by chance, was it fate?

He's a doctor now and I'm a nurse trying to heal a troubled people, both Israeli and Palestinian.

We have a son now and hope he grows up in a peaceful land.

I was in a bunker during my first war at his age!

We have given him both an Israeli and Palestinian name.

For balance, Mama used to say.

For peace.

Salem and Salih, non-religious names we think?

Hope his school pals don't shorten the names to 'Sal'!

Finally, your emerald pendant did bring me luck as I knew it would.

It saved my life I'm told; so, thank you.

I'm now wearing a replica Mama bought for my 21st.

So, goodbye for now.

I'm enclosing my email address.

Who knows, you may visit Israel again and meet your Grandson?

Next year in Jerusalem?

Your loving daughter,

Shalom,

Inbar

Liam sat in the lounge for a long time re-reading the letter. He nearly missed the photograph stuck in the packet. A baby boy, his Grandson. He could see Sarah in his smile, pale gold flecks in his eyes. The letter grew sodden in his hands; his Sarah gone, so long again. But this time ...

'So long.' For good.

He knew then that he had another journey to make. From Ireland where they met to Israel to say goodbye. He would lay a stone on Sarah's grave, as was the tradition in Judaism. For permanence. He would buy a kippah, a skull cap. He would recite the kaddish in his mind, a silent respect. He would be Jewish for a day. And more, if we live beyond our days, for eternity.

He would forever have a foothold in two countries. In two worlds.

ABOUT THE AUTHOR

Michael bowler was born in Cahersiveen, Co. Kerry, Ireland.
He emigrated to England where he worked with Customs and Excise. From 1997 to 2013 he represented UK Customs in the world police and fire games as a middle-distance athlete. He also ran for Ireland in European and world master athletic championships.
Hence his mantra: I'm a runner not a writer'!
He is now retired on the iconic ring of Kerry with his collie 'Zebo' and jack russell 'Missy'.

Also, by the author:
Destiny of Dreams – ISBN 978-1853710650
Set in County Kerry in the 1950s, a magical childhood matures into a life beset by religious doubts, awakening sexuality and the raging loneliness of adolescence.

The Last Season – ISBN 978-1782377931
A collection of short stories.